2200

A STORY FOR THE TIMES

michele aikens

as told by *em ann ross*

Published by Clear Sight Coaching & Consulting Inc.
Copyright © 2025 by Michele Aikens

ISBN (paperback): 978-1-736-78524-9

For Onyx, from Bibi

Remember...

introduction

This story was a hobby, a place for my mind to play and to escape from what was happening in the world. I started writing this story in January of 2021. The things I saw and felt created a stress I had never experienced before. What was happening in the world seemed to be colliding with the painful, horrible history of our country. As a Believer, I also saw the collision of race (a man-made construct) and my faith. I needed to do something that would help make sense of what I was feeling. For three years I occasionally came back to this story to imagine the characters and where their struggles might take them. In 2024, I realized *2200* might be a place for more than just me to imagine. As I retreated from the news reports and the tension of society, I realized that this writing was my Holy Resistance.

I resist the idea that as a people we are powerless to impact the present and the future. Our wisdom is unique; carved out of systemic oppression. From the scraps we were given came a genius that solved problems and created beauty and art. Consider the inventions, patents, and literature attributed to those whose ancestors picked cotton, tobacco, sugar cane and more. Consider the writings of those whose ancestors were forbidden to learn to read. My Holy Resistance is to not bow to an oppressive system and its narrative, but to remind us that we are a people of solutions.

2200 is a story for the times, both the times we live, and prayerfully, for the future. *2200* is also a story for the generations; the aged, the active and the aspiring. Imagine with me the innovation and mindset necessary to create what becomes the Commune of African Descendants in *2200*. Does that mindset exist today? Or are we still hailing back to the mindset of the regrettable actions by the old African communities who sold their brothers and sisters into slavery? Those nations have apologized for what they didn't know would happen. The beneficiaries of the slave trade, however, have yet to acknowledge the source of their privilege and wealth. We who are here today see the effect of the murder and disenfranchisement of our people that I believe has a direct spiritual tie to the past. Might the thinking of the elders, as in this story, offer solutions for the problems today and in the future?

2200 is a generational story that crosses time. I pray it creates a hunger in you for a better world right where you live today. I also pray that you find your mothers, fathers, aunts, uncles and grandparents, and ask them what they're thinking. The answers to our struggles in the present and our children's needs for the future are sitting among us in seed form today. Those seeds are the insistent questions you must answer, the ideas you have been reticent to employ, and the dreams within you that birth vision and action. But those seeds also require death to reproduce.

Your fears must die. Your sense of inferiority must die. Your procrastination must die. Your sense of living only for yourself must die. There are a people at stake. What seed will you sow today for the future of them?

"I tell you the solemn truth, unless a kernel of wheat falls into the ground and dies, it remains a single kernel; but if it dies it produces a great harvest."
John 12:24

You are loved,

Michele Aikens

chapter 1: jason

Jason stands on a busy corner, brazenly selling drugs at dusk. Two other men stand back, watching him and looking out for police. There are none to be seen in this neighborhood. An addict stumbles away from Jason hastily inspecting the package and then looks over his shoulder. Two boys about nine years old play nearby and occasionally stop and mimic Jason's gestures and stance.

Something is wrong, Jason thought. His instincts had kept him out of trouble so far. All his peers had been caught, either by some undercover policeman still green enough to think arresting one street dealer would stem the flow of drugs, or by a rival's bullet in the acquisition of expanded territory. His crew took bets on when his *spidey sense* would run out, but in five years of dealing, it hadn't failed him once.

"Time to close up shop," he said to the two men standing back. He looked at the two children and said, "You played more than you watched the car. Here's $20.00. Make sure you spend it on some food. Now go home. I'll watch."

Jason watched the two boys until they were out of sight and then nodded to his friends. They got in the car and drove away, just as a black jeep with tinted windows pulled in down the street.

Rico and Monster were Jason's closest crew members. They were the only ones who knew where he lived. The bond of trust between them had been established since all three were in kindergarten.

Rico was the "pretty boy" in the trio. The ladies loved him, and his easy-going personality disarmed the instincts of both police officers and rivals. Rico was also the most lethal of the three. Jason had seen him hum as he sliced a man's throat. Monster, on the other hand, was more intimidating physically but a real sweetheart, as they often teased him. Monster was a big man who could often be seen slipping money to a bum or a child when he thought no one was looking. Monster didn't use weapons to kill a man; he preferred using his hands. He also had an uncanny insight into what motivated a person's actions. He was rarely surprised by betrayals and always knew who on the team would turn, often before they were even approached. When Monster got a feeling about someone, he wrote their name down and put it in a sealed envelope. The names of those who attempted to make deals behind their backs or sell them out were always in Monster's envelope. His nickname had nothing to do with his street persona but was given to him by Rico in fourth grade because he liked cookies so much. When they started in business, the 'Cookie' was dropped.

Monster pulled the car in front of Jason's apartment building.

"You good?" Rico asked.

Jason got out of the car and looked back. "See you later." He quickly walked up to the second-floor condominium, took a deep breath, and unlocked the door. Grandma was cooking; that meant she felt better. Jason breathed a sigh of relief.

Jason lived with his grandmother. Grandma Ruby had a bad heart, that is what the doctor told him. She had two heart attacks in the last two years, mainly because she would not stop doing for others. Ruby Sanders had lived in the neighborhood since 1954. Her folks saved money to move from the South and bought the two-flat on the south side. Ruby was an only child, and she had only one child, Jason's mother. Jason teased his grandmother about trying to re-make their family into a large one. She took in strays – people mostly, but occasionally a dog. If she heard about a neighbor in trouble, she took food. Mother needed a babysitter? Everyone knew Ruby loved children. But the children, strays, cooking, volunteering at the church and everything else Ruby did had taken a toll on her health. Ruby was 86 years old, but when everyone tried to get her to slow down after her first heart attack, she told them she "would rather wear out than rust out." Most folk just left her alone, except Jason. Jason had acquaintances, and even a friend or two, but Ruby was all the family he had. Hearing her hum put him in a great mood.

"Grandma!", he said with feigned annoyance, "I thought you were supposed to be resting today."

Ruby liked this game they played when she was feeling well.

"Don't give me no mess boy. Just sit down and eat!"

Jason kissed his grandmother on the top of her head and led her to the table. She had prepared a feast of smothered chicken with rice and green beans. Yes, Ruby felt good.

They sat down, and he told her all about his day at the factory where she thought he worked. After dinner, he kissed Ruby on the cheek and told her he would be back in a couple of hours. Ruby held him an extra-long time. Jason thought for a minute, perhaps he should stay in today. Then he shrugged off the thought, got his keys and his cell phone and went out to meet Rico and Monster for the evening shift.

The black jeep pulled to a stop, paying attention to the shift change on the corner. The driver and his passenger held the picture next to the light on the dash. The tinted windows kept anyone from seeing their faces or what they were doing. The scar that ran from his ear to the top corner of Jay's mouth seemed to change color in the dim light and give him an even more ominous appearance.

Butch compared the picture with the young man standing on the corner. "That's him. We need to do it quick. Right now, there are just two of them, but in 10 minutes the whole crew will be here."

"Let's go," Jay said in a low voice.

"What about the other one?", Tiny asked from the back seat.

"We'll use the taser on him and leave. We only want the main guy.

The three men in the car pulled ski masks over their heads. Two exited the car moving stealthily under the cover of dark. As the target finished outlining the evening's assignments and all except one walked away, Jay moved in behind one of them and tased him as Butch put a bag over the other man's head and shoved him into the back seat of the jeep.

No one noticed what happened until the truck pulled away from the curb. The whole thing took less than a minute. Butch placed a call to the number, said one word and hung up: "Done."

chapter 2: althea

The woman leaned back and took another sip of the fresh-squeezed beet juice. The sun was warm on her face as she surveyed the exquisite outdoor space. After family meditation, they each went to their favorite parts of the house for alone time. This was her spot; the sun warmed her bones, and the sounds of wind, water and birds soothed her mind. Althea was grateful. Today her family really heard her as she spoke passionately about their duty to the past. They had an important decision to make this week.

In the 21st century around the year 2030, the Sixth Amendment to the U.S. Constitution was repealed by the Twenty-eighth Amendment. The Sixth Amendment guaranteed the right to legal representation, trial by jury and other things thought to be cumbersome in the fight against crime. Politicians and large corporations formed open partnerships to stop violent crime by insuring those convicted of these crimes were immediately taken off the streets permanently. Unlike in previous attempts to stand up for the accused, there was no public outcry. The community had grown tired of the murders and disregard for life. Those committing the crimes were not moved by the tears of mothers, sisters, and children. And those who had once advocated for the accused were no longer moved by the plight of those arrested. The Community had grown exhausted.

Convicted persons who weren't immediately executed after being judged guilty were transported to work camps where the very corporations that lobbied for the laws, now enjoyed the privilege of free labor. Young Black men who were known to be involved in violent crime were picked up without warrants and placed in jail. To expedite justice, those whose families could afford lawyers could risk a trial, but if the son was found guilty, there were no appeals but immediate deportation to work camp for the rest of their natural lives, or execution.

For those families willing to risk significant resources and bet on the future, however, there was a third option. Family Futures, Inc. (FFI), a biotechnology company that had won the biggest share of the human cryotechnology research market, offered families willing to pay the chance to have their convicted sons preserved for four generations, 160 years, and then entrusted to future descendants. This option was considered more humane than death or life as a corporate slave because it gave the convicted criminal the chance at a future. The criminal's family in the future would have to incur the expense of waking him up, housing, and incorporating him into their lives. The future family could also choose to disconnect the relative from the life support system and let him terminate, or for additional fees, let the relative sleep for the next generation to decide. The maximum time allowed for sleepers was 200 years. 200 years. Only a third of the families with relatives entrusted to them through cryotechnology ever woke their relatives up;

most preferred to not upset the family balance by living with a convicted criminal as part of their legacy. If there was a family stalemate, they paid for the sleeper to be kept for an additional 40 years, kicking the proverbial "can down the road" for the next generation to deal with.

Althea Akachi received notice a month ago that a relation from before was approaching his time. She remembered the heated discussion 40 years prior that kept him in cryosleep for an additional 40 years. He had been kept the maximum amount of time; the family had to decide to wake him up or let him terminate. As the family matriarch, the official notice had come to her, and it was her responsibility to persuade the family to give a second chance at life to one of their own. She leaned over and opened the large envelope to look at the profile of their relative again.

He was handsome. She could see similar features in her son, who was the same age as the man in the picture, twenty-four. Yes, he was family. She looked at the papers in the envelope. Convicted drug dealer. That wasn't even a crime outside the commune anymore. Althea tried to imagine his mother and grandmother. She closed her eyes and calmly asked God what she should do. The still, small voice responded: "Go get him."

Nicholas Amare loved his mother. Althea was good and wise. However, Nick didn't believe getting the relative from before was the right decision. Rescuing a relation from the past would throw the family into even greater turmoil.

Mom was one of the most respected elders in their commune, but she had become soft and emotional in her later years. Nicholas also knew that Althea was thinking of transitioning out of the advisory commune and into the community of elders and children. While Nicholas was the obvious choice to replace Althea, there were others in the family who wanted the position of Family Elder. Nicholas wanted to protect the family from what he believed to be a bad decision. Integrating a newcomer into their lives would further upset their tenuous family bonds.

Nicholas also believed his mother had another motive for waking the sleeper. Though powerful, their clan was one of the smallest in the Community of African Descendants. Althea wanted grandchildren, and if the sleeper could acclimate and find a mate, their family line would grow. Currently Nicholas was Althea's only direct heir, and having a family simply wasn't a priority to him. If the awakened relative could acclimate into the family and community and find a suitable mate, he could give Althea the grandchildren she longed for. As a direct heir with offspring, he would also be eligible to assume the role of Family Elder, though that had never happened.

Integrating *the sleepers from before* usually presented problems – either for the sleepers, or for the family that took them in. First there was the issue of the sleeper adapting to a time up to 200 years in the future. Everything about life had changed and many sleepers, realizing that all those they knew were dead, opted for the self-elimination meds.

If the sleeper decided to remain with their family, he or she would have to be integrated into their daily lives. The newly integrated family member, according to communal law, had to be allocated a portion of the family's inheritance and treated as if he were a part of their lives from the beginning. This usually presented a problem for current family members who had to relinquish part of their inheritance to the new family member. Finally, the relative had been put to sleep in the first place because of criminal behavior. Often the criminal behavior resurfaced, making it impossible for the new family to acclimate the sleeper to their way of life. The solution to the problem of returning criminal behavior was release from the Commune of African Descendants to the outside.

Because responsibility had been passed to their generation, it became the head of the family's responsibility to terminate their relative from the past prior to waking or release the sleeper into the world beyond the commune. This was not taken lightly and was only allowed after bringing the sleeper before the Council of Families, the judicial arm over all families in the commune of African Descendants. If a sleeper was released into the world outside the commune, he was given a stipend, enough to find housing, and identifying paperwork. After being released, it was on the sleeper to make his or her own way in a world vastly different than the one they had known. It was the harshest of punishments and only done as a last resort because the relative to be released was, ironically, the reason for the current wealth of his or her family.

If a sleeper was terminated prior to waking, the Council of Family Elders administered the execution. Each Council Member was responsible for administering a portion of the dosage, so both *no one and all were responsible.*

The Council of Families had unique authority in this area because of the deal made with Family Futures, Incorporated. Were it not for the African American families who allowed their families to be the experimental subjects, FFI, and all programs like it would not exist. In exchange for the young men and women who became sleepers under the FFI program, the government agreed to give the Council of Families jurisdiction over all those who had been awakened in the future. This jurisdiction, in addition to the significant financial investment in those families, resulted in a new way of living for those formerly referred to as African Americans. The response to this new authority was a change in how African American communities were managed. The changes were noticeable socially, economically, and even physically.

As the influence of the Council of Families grew, the community turned even more inward, educating its young, creating economic systems that nurtured growth, and even changing dietary standards. The result was a 0-2% crime rate, no poverty and unemployment, and a noticeable change in the physical attributes of those living within the Commune of African Descendants. When crime did happen within the commune, it was always the result of an awakened sleeper who couldn't acclimate.

Nicholas knew all of this. He also knew that if Althea went to get their new relative, that relative would become his responsibility. With everything happening, including his potential assumption of Althea's role as Family Head and representative to the advisory council, Nick knew that any consequences of waking the relative would be his to unravel. He understood that as Family Elder his role was also to preserve and ensure the success of families within the commune – past, present, and future. This built-in conflict was the calling and burden of every leader in the commune. He looked at his timepiece. It was time for the meeting with his mother.

chapter 3: the farm

It was time to wake up the trainees. The old man rang a bell that could be heard all over the compound. It was 4:30 AM. Will walked to the large barn where the trainees lived and inspected the dormitory. There were twenty-four twin-sized beds placed twelve on each side of the barn and a desk at the very back of the barn for the watchman.

The watchman's job was to make sure the trainees slept. They were not to fight, talk, attempt to have sex with each other or create a hierarchy of any kind. Just sleep. This place was where reprogramming happened. Will walked to the back of the barn and sat on the desk, talking quietly to Rufus.

"Did you have any trouble last night?"

Rufus shook his head. Since the incident last week, there had been no talk of rebellion or attempts at uprising.

Last week was the first real test for the organization called simply, "The Farm." The Farm was a network of rural dormitories in the south, completely off the grid, that held some of the most violent men from the streets of America. Each farm in the network housed between 25 and 100 men in military-styled barracks. The men were overseen by other armed men, and those men had even less to lose than those they had snatched off the streets. While on The Farm, trainees were required to work, either in the fields, the kitchens, mending fences, building dormitories or whatever task was assigned.

Each farm in the network, in addition to planting crops, furnished something for the other farms. Clothing was manufactured in Tennessee, while cabinetry and small carpentry work were done in Georgia. Plumbers were trained in South Carolina and dispatched under careful supervision to the other farms as needed. No one collected a salary. Gangsters, drug dealers and other violent members of African American communities nationally were brought to The Farm for reprogramming, protection and re-education.

The Farm was a way of life these detainees had never experienced. For some, the discipline, labor, and behavioral restrictions were too much, and a few needed medical attention. Just last week, one of the inmates had tried to run. Will and Rufus laughed quietly as they remembered. The poor guy, who said his nickname was "Killer," was only familiar with city streets, not the country. The fella just took off running when the crew had a break and Rufus wasn't looking. Killer didn't know north from south, or east from west. He ran until he saw a truck carrying plumbing equipment, flagged it down and asked to be taken to the nearest city. The driver of the truck was from Georgia, and recognized the uniform as one of the Mississippi farm trainees. Fortunately for Rufus, the driver brought young Killer right back to the farm. They may not be so fortunate next time. The team would have to keep tighter rein on the trainees. That was a discussion for the next meeting, but now it was time to oversee the work.

Each dormitory housed twenty-four men; and there were four dormitories on the Mississippi farm. Rufus and Will were responsible for the newest group. As the men progressed after three months, they were transferred to other leaders. Every man did a minimum of one year on the farm unless he died during the process. The first three months on the farm were the hardest because the first three months were designed to instill discipline. The men on The Farm weren't used to discipline or hard physical labor. They were accustomed to creating opportunities to dominate others while advancing their own agenda. These men were accustomed to identifying the weak and exploiting them to accomplish their sinister goals. The rules on The Farm were few and strict during the first months of training:

1. Get up when we tell you.
2. Eat what you are given.
3. No talking
4. Sit where you are told
5. Finish eating by 5:00 am
6. Start work in the fields at 5:15 am
7. Don't try to leave.
8. Don't ask questions. You'll know when it's time for you to know.

Jason felt like he had been thrown into scme Negro spiritual slave novel. He remembered the long ride with his head covered. Everything happened so fast: guys with masks and tasers, Monster collapsing like a little girl and someone putting a bag over his head and a needle in his arm. When he woke up, he was in some old slave quarters-looking building that smelled like what he suspected was manure. It was hot. His clothes were gone, and he was in some kind of prison outfit.

A man who said his name was Will told him he was on a farm in Mississippi, and that he would be there for a year unless he died. His job was to harvest cane. What the hell was that?

When he asked Will if he meant "cocaine," Will said, "Naw boy. Sugar cane."

This was surreal. He didn't understand what was going on. He heard animal sounds.

"Come on boy. Dem's the cows coming, which means it's time for dinner. Come on and I'll get you fed too."

Jason said, "Uh, sir, I have an aunt that I take care of and she's sickly. She will be worried about me. May I at least call her and let her know I'm ok?"

Will looked at him and said coldly, "You should have thought about your sick Grandma Ruby while you were selling drugs. Now get to the mess hall."

chapter 4: ruby

Ruby hadn't slept much last night. Jason didn't come home, and she knew that she would probably never see him again. She didn't believe his lies for one moment about a factory job – one look at Jason's hands would tell anyone he didn't work in nobody's factory. Who did he think he was talking to? She had known for about a year that her grandbaby was one of the biggest drug dealers in the neighborhood.

To his credit, he didn't sell to children from what she could glean, and he had never killed anyone. She wasn't so sure about those two friends of his, though. She stirred the tea absentmindedly while looking out of the window. She wondered where he was at this moment and what he must be feeling. Ruby also wondered if she had made the right decision. She had a pain in her chest, forcing her to stop and breathe deeply. If she held her breath the pain would pass eventually. The medicine was no longer working, and Ruby knew her days were coming to an end. She worried so much about Jason. He was a good boy that got caught up in the streets after his parents left. Maybe she should have. Her thoughts were interrupted by a loud knock on the apartment door.

"Open up. Police. We have a warrant."

Ruby walked slowly to the door. Yes, she had done the right thing.

chapter 5: althea

Althea rose from her seat at the meeting of the Council of Elders of African Descendants. Her family was at a stalemate; divided down the middle on whether to wake their relative from before. Those opposed to waking him were led by her son, Nicholas. He argued persuasively about preserving the gains made by not allowing influences from the past to dilute their present progress. Althea knew that his real concern would be the dilution of his influence and the potential challenge to his assumed leadership role after she moved to the commune of elders and children. Her heart cried as she understood that by his stance, her son had demonstrated himself unfit to lead in her stead. Those serving as Elders were required to have respect for the entire story of Descendants of Africans, not just the current reality. Althea sadly accepted that she would not be able to leave the Council of Families until someone could be found to take her place.

Leaving the family compound, Althea walked through the gate leading into the commune of elders and children. She caught her breath at the sound of children singing. Oh, how she missed that sound! She followed the path that led to the history corridor and took a seat on a bench outside the learning room where she could hear the lesson.

She closed her eyes:

Before, the old were relegated to centers where they deteriorated mentally and physically. But in the Commune of Elders and Children, the greatest minds in the community educated the youngest minds. The changes seen in the Commune of African Descendants can be directly attributed to the interaction between the oldest and the youngest in the community. The elderly had a sense of purpose in investing in the future, and the youngest grew to love, respect, and depend on the knowledge of the elders.

Althea sat outside listening to the interaction and wiped silent tears. She would not join the Commune of Elders and Children for a while.

The issue of their sleeping relative was going to be a difficult and divisive one for her family. She was needed on the Council of Family Elders until a compassionate replacement from her own family could be found. Shaking herself, she got up from the bench and made her way back to the meeting place for the Council of Elders. It was time.

Meetings of the Council of Family Elders were a solemn occasion. Children aged 12 and over were allowed seating in a special session with their instructors where they could quietly observe the proceedings. The gallery was open to all members of the Commune of African Descendants, but the decisions of the Council of Family Elders overruled all family arguments and opinions; each family as part of their residence in the Commune of African Descendants submitted to this order. There were some African Descendants who found life within the Commune too restrictive, so they lived outside among the masses. Life for them was essentially as it had been for people of color at the turn of the 21st century

Althea was the last to take her place on the dais as prayers were offered by the Lead Elder, Elijah Chikelu. The Lead Elder represented the largest family within the Commune, but all Elders had equal say in the affairs of the Council. Chikelu opened the meeting:

"We are here to discuss and determine the outcome of importance to our families and our community. The seeds of the past, with which we have been entrusted today, are once again in our hands.

Three of our families have been given the responsibility to repair the stain of the past with the prospect of new life today. You have discussed among yourselves, and we, as your Council of Elders, will hear your decisions and resolve any conflicts. Let us all repeat our promise to each other: 'The past made us blood, the present makes us family, the future makes us stronger so long as we remain one. Amen.'"

The families brought their decisions to the Council one by one, with Elijah asking the same question of them all.

"First the Folami Family. Please stand. How does your clan decide?"

"To the Elders, our family has chosen to wait a generation before waking our son."

Elijah: "And your clan is in agreement with this?"

Folami: "Yes, Elder, we are in agreement."

Elijah: "So be it. Your relative will sleep for another generation. Thank you for your unity."

Elijah: "Now the Jabari Family. Please stand. How does your clan decide?"

Jabari: "To the Elders, our family has chosen to terminate our son."

Elijah: "You have chosen the irrevocable option of termination. As required by our agreement, we must poll each of your Family Elders to insure this is a unified decision. Jabari Clan, please stand for questioning."

chapter 6: the farm

Jason kept his head down and tried not to draw attention to himself as he walked in line with the others. For some reason it seemed all eyes were on him since he had arrived last week. Will, the man in charge of watching over them at night, let everyone know that Jason had overseen a drug selling operation. The other inmates, upon hearing this, wanted to bring him down a notch, while those in charge singled him out for special mistreatment. Jason didn't understand what was happening. He was anxious about Ruby – she was sick, alone and no doubt worried. Yes, he sold drugs and had a successful operation. He had never been caught by the police, so he didn't understand how he ended up in this place.

"You, drug dealer," a man named Allan called out. "We need you to help us expand this room. Will, send the drug dealer and four of those others back here."

Will looked at Jason and the other men with him. "Well, it ain't killin' your people. Let's see how you do with some good old-fashioned hard work. Go on over to Allan."

Allan was talking to some of the other older men in charge about a new group coming in this evening. "We need to push the room back 40 feet and build walls. Then we need to accommodate the extra beds here," he said pointing to an open field. "I just got word the bus carrying the next load is full, so we have to hustle. I'll take this one with me.

The rest of them can get started chopping and cutting wood."

Allan turned and walked towards the pick-up truck, gesturing for Jason to follow him. When they were just out of sight of the camp, Allan turned to Jason and punched him twice in the face, knocking him to the ground. "That's just in case you ever get a notion to try me. I also carry a gun. Get in the truck."

chapter 7: ruby

"No officer, I haven't seen my grandson in a week. Do you know where he is? Do you have him in custody?"

"Ma'am, we are here because we have a warrant for your grandson's arrest, and this is his last known residence. We are going to search your house now. Just sit here and if you have nothing to hide, this will be over soon."

Ruby sat on the couch and watched the officers turn Jason's room upside down. She heard the bureau hit the floor and wondered how she was going to put that upright. She started to sweat, and her arm hurt. Absentmindedly she rubbed her arm as she thought about what to do next. There were no drugs here. Rico and Big Sheldon came by the night Jason got taken and took everything incriminating out of the house. Ruby stayed in the kitchen cooking and had no idea what those boys took. Rico promised to check in on her and said to let him know if anyone came by. Big Sheldon offered to sleep on the couch, but Ruby would have none of that. That big boy would ruin her couch. She supposed they called him Monster for a reason. *Snap out of it Ruby!* she thought. *What's your next move?*

After what seemed like hours the officers addressed her: "Here's a card. Would you call us if your grandson comes home or if you hear from him?"

Assuring them that she would most certainly do her duty and call, she closed the door behind them.

Ruby hurried to the medicine cabinet to take one of her heart pills. There were only two left. She didn't have much time. She went into her room and got Jason's file. She packed a suitcase for a couple of days and quickly dressed to catch the bus to Detroit. She looked around her home for one last time. Ruby knew she wouldn't be coming back. This was necessary for her family's future. Jason was all she had left in the world, and she would protect him at all costs. A tear escaped from her eye and for a moment she thought to indulge the need to cry. Shaking off the urge, she looked around one last time, turned off the lights, and left the life she knew.

The bus pulled into the Detroit terminal right on time the next day. Ruby woke up as the sunlight hit her face. She still didn't feel good, but the overnight sleep on the bus helped refresh her. It was a short cab ride to FFI. She hoped it wasn't too late to be part of the experiment. When she got into the waiting room she looked around. Everyone in there was at least 65 and many were much older. Just like her, these people were putting their hopes in the future. Those in the waiting room couldn't tell their families for fear of being called old and crazy, not that Ruby had anyone needing an explanation. Her money was hers to do as she pleased, and she was betting it all. Ruby registered her name and took a seat.

chapter 8: the farm

Allan and Jason rode in silence. After getting in the truck, Allan made Jason change his shirt to one that was on the seat. After a while, Allan said, "I imagine you have a lot of questions. You won't get any other opportunities, so I suggest you ask them now."

Jason's mind was reeling, and he didn't know where to start. He decided to go for the obvious: "Where am I?"

"You're on The Farm. The Farm is a network of rural re-training centers spread throughout the South and Midwest. It was created to save our people by taking the most dangerous elements in our communities off the streets."

"Retraining?" Jason raised his eyebrows. "You mean reprogramming? Because it seems you are treating our people like slaves. I don't understand."

Allan interrupted, "Do you want to have a discussion or try to convince me that you don't belong here?" Allan patted his pocket as a reminder of their earlier conversation. "Reprogramming might be a better term," he continued. "You and others like you in our world have lost your sense of respect for yourselves and each other. You have bought into the capitalist mindset that you must get money by any means possible. Even if those means are to sell drugs, shoot up our communities or steal and rob. This behavior is not only harmful in the short run, but you who are here, are destroying our future. The Farm is the solution.

Some of the men in charge here were like you – criminals and destroyers who were taught by other men the value of life, family, and community. Others were in business, tradesmen, lawyers. We even have some former police officers. Those were the things we did in our former lives, before we got old and started thinking about how we would leave the world. The men here are investing the rest of their lives in reminding men who they were created to be. It seems hard to you because some of you have never experienced the strong discipline of another man. You were raised by women who did their best, but in their attempts to make up for what society did to you, they made you soft and entitled. You knew it was wrong inside, which is why you responded to the women in your life with such disrespect. Your entitlement has landed you here on The Farm.”

Jason was stunned. “My grandmother Ruby. She is sick. I’m the only family she has. She will be worried,” Jason stammered.

Allan’s next words chilled Jason to his bones: “Your grandmother knows you’re on The Farm. Nobody is here without their nearest relative’s permission. Now we’re at the supply store. Don’t try anything stupid.” Allan patted his pocket where he had the gun and nodded for Jason to get out.

chapter 9: althea

Althea's heart was beating fast. While all the Family Elders in the clan agreed to wake up the son, Nick expressed his disagreement vehemently in the meeting. The other elders went along with her decision, though two were reluctant. Chief Elder Chikelu fixed his gaze on Althea, sensing her concern. Nevertheless, it was time to call her family. Althea rose and faced the elders:

Elijah: "Now the Akachi Family. Please stand. How does your clan decide?"

Althea Akachi: "To the Elders, our family has chosen to awaken our son."

Elijah: "And your entire clan is in agreement with this decision?"

Akachi: "Yes, Elder we are in agreement."

Elijah: "So be it. Your son will be awakened to join his family and our world. Thank you for your unity."

Nick was furious. Not only did his mother blatantly ignore all of his arguments against waking up the criminal, but she humiliated him in front of all the elders by making him feel like a child. She didn't even leave room for him to speak! How was he to be respected as her successor if his opinions were treated so casually? Althea knew that if Nick spoke out against her wishes in the presence of the assembled, he would never be considered for the position of Family Elder.

The council valued unity above all other virtues. For centuries, their descendants had been intentionally separated by things as trite as neighborhoods, skin color, or educational status. The Community of African Descendants worked to build unity from the least to the greatest in every family within the commune. The most effective leaders in the Community were those who were able to foster unity. Nick knew that one word spoken against the decision would mark him as one who could not be trusted with the unity of the family. He would just have to prove his mother wrong by keeping track of the *new son*. When that son inevitably went the way of the other criminals, Nick would be there as the voice of reason. He would be vindicated as leader, and his mother could be sent to join the Elder's and Children's commune.

Nick practiced a smile he didn't feel. The preparations for the Awakening started as soon as the Council adjourned.

Back in her private space, Althea replayed the day. She sensed a rift between her and Nick that might never heal. His arguments against waking their son were motivated by his desire to become Family Elder unchallenged, and sole heir to all their family fortune. Ironically, it was his disposition concerning family that challenged his position as Family Elder. Adding a son would require the fortune be allocated to them both, and although it had never happened with one of the awakened, the new son could become an heir after his time of proving. Althea prayed silently for Nick's heart to be healed of the need to rule.

Rulership was not a position to covet, but an opportunity to serve. She also prayed for their new son who would be joining them in a matter of days. Preparations had to be made. Althea shook off the sadness and got up to prepare the living quarters for the new son.

chapter 10: the farm

The men sitting in the store playing checkers stopped talking when Jason and Allan came in.

"Good to see you, Allan. You got somebody new with you today?"

Jason couldn't tell if the store owner was being friendly or nosy. He had been instructed not to speak to anyone and to stick near Allan.

"Yes," Allan replied. "A new trainee for the construction program."

"Hey, how do I get my boys in that training program?" Jason noticed that the men stopped pretending and stared at Allan.

"All the men in this program are here on special scholarship. Besides, I don't handle that part of things." Allan looked at Jason, "Make sure you get everything on this list."

The store owner side-eyed Jason and Allan as he filled their baskets. Another man loaded a circular saw into the back of the truck. Allan nodded to the men playing checkers as they walked out the door. Jason could feel the eyes and animosity of those men on their backs as they left. The sense he had on the streets kicked in- these men wanted trouble at The Farm.

Back in the truck, Jason asked Allan everything he could think of: "What was The Farm, and how did it get started?"

Allan patiently answered all of his questions, filling in the blanks until Jason understood what was happening. The Farm was a network started by older African Americans who had unused land in the south. These elders, recognizing the crises of crime, violence, and loss of care within the African American community, started talking among themselves about what could be done. At first the conversations were held among the older members within families, but soon the families began to connect until there was a network of elders that was countrywide. Discreetly, they met in church basements, at senior citizens Bingo games, and in corners at community barbecues where they were mostly left alone. They discussed what could be done to help their grandchildren, great grandchildren and others find their way. One older man from Detroit made a comment about taking the biggest criminal elements, many who had the brightest minds, from the community "down South" to be reacquainted with what's important: hard work, care for family and community, and building for a future. He half-jokingly said, "I have 37 acres of land just sitting in Mississippi, and I would give it up if someone had an idea of how to use it." There were others like him, hundreds, that had left land in the south for a better life in the north.

In 2030 when the sixth amendment was repealed, their casual conversations took on a serious and hurried tone. If they were going to help the young people, it had to happen now.

Under the guise of farming, manufacturing and trades work, the elders signed their land over to a corporation called, The Farm, Incorporated. In exchange for their donation of land, an elder could call the surveillance team and have a person picked up and taken to The Farm. Those taken disappeared without a trace, usually off the streets at night. A short message was sent to the elder relative or caller confirming the pick-up. The Farm had been in operation, right under the noses of the government, for more than two years. In that time, hundreds of young Black men had returned to their communities changed, having learned a trade or skill from which their families could be supported. A hundred or so left the farm to return to the criminal lives they lived, and most were now in prison workhouses where they would live until they died. Those who weren't in workhouses got the benefit of the twenty-eighth Amendment: execution once convicted. Sixty of the young men who were captured elected to stay on The Farm and be trained to eventually take over.

"I'm telling you this, Jason, because we have been watching you. I hope that you will stay and become part of this, but drug dealers have the worst survival rate at The Farm. There's something about the easy money, and the sense of entitlement that makes this process harder for them. Nobody is going to give you a pass or make it easy for you, but now you know why. You're a leader, and leaders have a different kind of proving ground. We're almost back, so we'll have to talk another time. Just keep your head down and do what you're told."

Pulling back into the farm compound, Jason looked at Allan and asked, "You mean my grandmother knew about this?"

Allan looked at Jason and laughed. "Boy, you're on your grandmother's land. Now start unloading the truck."

chapter 11: ruby

Ruby's head was light with relief as she pushed the elevator button. She had done it. She had safeguarded her grandson's life no matter what happened. She signed the contract with FFI, and paid them all she had. After the legal and financial things were done, Ruby got to write a letter to Jason. That was the hardest part of the day, because she knew it meant she would never see her grandson again. Walking off the elevator, still carrying the overnight bag, she wondered where she would go. Should she try to catch a bus back to Chicago or get a room for the night and leave in the morning. Feeling light and happy, she realized she didn't have to decide. She could have lunch, sit in the beautiful park, and check the bus schedule.

There was a park across the street with a restaurant and a fountain. Ruby felt dizzy as she considered everything that had happened. She made her way to a bench in front of the water fountain. *I'll just catch my breath and get my bearings,* she thought. *And then I'm going to treat myself to a fancy lunch at that restaurant.*

Rico and Monster had been watching Jason's house non-stop since he disappeared. They both knew that if he were alive, he would find a way to see his grandmother. This didn't look good. Jason had been gone for more than three months without a trace.

Their crews were gathering intel from around the city, and it seemed legitimate. Nobody knew what happened to Jason. Monster was confused because this didn't make sense. Rico was scared, and now Ruby was missing.

The two friends went into the house, discreetly, to see what they could find. Both of them said it together: "Ruby knew she wouldn't be back."

Now it was serious. They searched the house looking for a clue as to where Ruby and Jason had gone. Monster found a brochure for a startup company in Detroit that had an appointment time. Rico found a copy of an old deed to a parcel of land in Mississippi. So Ruby owned land in Mississippi. Could she have gone there without saying anything?

The two friends decided to continue paying the rent on the small apartment knowing that if Jason was alive, he would come back here.

chapter 12: althea

She hoped the new son would like his quarters. She had read the history of life during his time on a number of occasions. Althea wanted to create an atmosphere of peace and calm in contrast to what he remembered. She prayed silently as she remembered the struggles to adjust by those who were awakened. Normally she and Nicholas, as immediate family, would spend large amounts of time with the new son, but Althea wasn't holding out hope for Nicholas' participation.

She situated the new son's quarters opposite Nicholas' with her quarters between theirs. Out of respect for Nicholas she chose to put as much space as allowed within their commune between the two of them. Althea didn't want to force them on each other, but instead hoped they would seek each other out. Nicholas preferred the evening sun, so the new son would get the early morning sun. She hoped that the rising sun of each new day would give him hope and gladness for the new life he had been given. As was custom in the commune, the awakened were simply referred to as "My son," "my brother," "my cousin," or "my nephew" until the end of the first year – the time of proving. The original elders did not want the awakened to be burdened with the shame of their former name, but to demonstrate characteristics over a year that would earn him or her a new name. The new naming was part of the official induction into the

Commune of African Descendants after a year of proving.

Althea allowed herself a moment to imagine her two sons connecting as brothers and carrying the family legacy forward peacefully. She daydreamed of their children playing together while her sons calmly built a legacy for their family side by side. She thought of their family colors which would be worn proudly at the induction, and of the naming ceremony for the son. She closed her eyes and whispered a prayer for unity in her family, and then she stopped as she heard whispers coming from another part of the family compound.

Althea could make out the voice of Nicholas as he spoke with another person. She could make out the whispered words,"losing her faculties," and movement to the "Commune of Transition." Althea paused. Was her beloved Nicholas, in his anger, attempting to discredit her as being mentally unstable? If he could convince a majority of the Family Elders that Althea was deteriorating mentally, they would agree to move her into the Commune of Transition; the final living place for those who were terminally ill and unable to serve the community. She placed her hand on the wall as tears of anger and betrayal began to flow. Althea and Nicholas had disagreed before, but the idea that her son would betray her to get his way was almost too much. It was almost enough to break her. But not enough. Althea wiped her eyes, steeled her composure, and finished creating the home within their quarters for the son she had yet to meet.

"It wasn't fair!" He was Althea's first born and only son. The position of Family Elder was rightfully his. No stranger from before had a right to disrupt the relationship between his mother and him. Althea must not be in her right mind to let a sleeper from the past disrupt the natural order. "Yes, that was it," he reasoned. His mother was in the early stages of diminished mental capacity; that is why she was so insistent on including a sleeper from the past into their family structure. There was no other explanation for her stubborn stance on waking the sleeper and upsetting the family's balance.

Nicholas needed the counsel of another elder; one not so smitten with his mother. Althea was greatly admired among the Council, so Nicholas had to be careful in choosing who to confide in. To terminate a family member from the past was privately frowned upon because the wealth of the Commune of African Descendants was a direct result of an ancestor agreeing to submit to the experimentation of cryosleep. The descendants believed terminating a sleeper was the ultimate act of ingratitude as it called for the murder of one tied directly to their current wealth. Nevertheless, Elder Benjamin, who had once faced the same choice as Althea, was able to persuade the Jabari Tribe to terminate their sleeper. Elder Benjamin was the man Nicholas would speak with.

Feigning concern for his mother's health, Nicholas explained to Elder Benjamin that his mother was in such a hurry to get to the Commune of Elders and Children that she wasn't thinking about the future of their family. He explained that Althea's insistence on waking the sleeper was inconsistent with her past behaviors and whispered that he felt she was not in control of her mental faculties.

Elder Benjamin was articulate and dignified. While others valued unity above all virtues, true to his name, Benjamin Jabari believed the best measure of courage was how willing one was to disagree with popular thought. Unknown to others, Benjamin had lucrative financial interests outside the Commune that he was not willing to give up. He found life inside the Commune of African Descendants slow and unexciting. He had known long ago that Althea would become the Chief Elder and pursued her romantically in hopes of sharing the inevitable power and influence she would wield. He even cultivated a relationship with her then teenage son in hopes of becoming Althea's husband, Nicholas' father, and ultimately sharing the power of the Chief Elder over the council. Althea saw through him and spurned his romantic efforts. Her rejection embarrassed and embittered him, and he promised himself he would return the favor one day. Apparently, that day was dawning.

chapter 14: the farm

The days and nights ran together as just one, long, never-ending bad dream. The daily drudgery, public humiliation for the smallest infraction, the loneliness. Worst of all was knowing that you were being scrutinized to see if you could make the leadership cut. It had been six months, as far as Jason could tell, since he was taken off the street. He had no word about his grandmother. Rico and Monster had not come for him. He was cut off from everything familiar. He turned over to try to sleep. He had gotten used to the quiet and now slipped into a deep, dreamless sleep at the end of each long day. Tonight was different though. Jason could not stop worrying about Ruby. He made up his mind he would talk to Allan in the morning. He just needed to know Ruby was alright.

***

The damn rooster was crowing already. It seemed Jason had just fallen asleep after tossing all night. Jason and the other men in the barracks stood up quietly, accustomed to the routine now, and dressed.

As they made their way to the outside, Allan pulled Jason aside. "We need to talk. Come with me."

In the Farmhouse, Jason was given a full breakfast, including coffee and juice. Allan sat down across from him.

"I'll get right to the point. We haven't heard from your grandmother and some of us are worried. You will be allowed to go and check on her, with an escort.

We leave after breakfast."

Jason was numb on the ride back to the city. In the six months he had been on The Farm he had apparently grown accustomed to the quiet. The city noises were jarring to him. More than the noise, though, he was worried – panicked even – about Ruby. Knowing those in charge of The Farm kept in touch with Ruby had given him a strange comfort. He knew that at least she was ok. Now he couldn't stop his mind from worrying about what she had been going through for the last six months. He dozed fretfully throughout the trip.

When Allan stopped the truck, Jason was wide awake at once.

Allan spoke sternly: "We know there is a warrant out for your arrest, and that the police have been here at least twice. We also know that the rent is being paid anonymously. You're not safe here, Jason, so don't get any ideas about slipping away. If you're not down here in 20 minutes, I'm leaving and you're on your own."

Jason considered Allan's warning for a minute and got out of the car without a word. Unrecognizable in the clothes given to him by The Farm, Jason slipped undetected into the building and up to the apartment he shared with his grandmother. They had given him the key that was in the clothes they had taken when he was abducted, so he let himself in. Standing in the living room, Jason realized — he couldn't *feel his grandmother*. She had not been here for a while. He checked the medicine cabinet; her medicine was gone. Looking in her room, he noticed an overnight bag missing, but her suitcase was still here.

The smell in the house was dusty and stale; no one had been here for some time. Walking into the kitchen, Jason was about to check the refrigerator when he heard the back door open and turned to look into the face of Monster. First, they stared for a few seconds as recognition dawned, and then Monster picked him up in a big bear hug.

"Where have you been? You've been gone for months without a word."

Before Jason could answer Rico walked through the open door, gently closing it.

"Y'all are too loud. This place is supposed to be empty, and empty means quiet." Rico wasn't happy. "We've been worried sick about you. Do you know how many people I had to…" Rico stopped. "Where have you been?"

"Sit down," Jason said. "But first, where's my grandmother?"

Monster looked at Rico. Rico looked at Jason and took a breath.

"Ruby died."

chapter 15: jason

Jason howled as if he had been struck. Rico turned away while Monster stood by. For six months Jason had wondered about the only family he had, only to come home and find out she died. The hardened street persona returned as if the past six months hadn't happened. Jason walked over to the cabinets and touched a handle. The last time he saw her she had felt well enough to cook.

"What happened?" Jason asked.

Monster poured water into the tea kettle while Rico guided Jason to the kitchen table.

"From what we can tell, Grandma Ruby met with some people at FFI in Detroit three months ago. We're not sure what that meeting was about, but when she didn't come home, we took a trip to Detroit to find out about FFI, and to look for her. It seemed like she just disappeared after her meeting, so we hired a detective. Did you know your grandmother had land in Mississippi?", Rico paused and asked.

Jason nodded absently.

Rico continued, "We started asking around the network about an 84-year-old woman who had recently met with FFI. Nobody knew anything until somebody remembered an elderly Jane Doe who died in the park right across from FFI."

Monster sat some of his grandmother's favorite peppermint tea on the table in front of him and then moved oddly far away from them both to the living room window.

"We went to the morgue and identified her. We picked out a nice plot in Detroit and had a quiet burial with just us. We didn't want to draw attention by bringing her here. I'm sorry, Jason. But where have you been?"

"It doesn't even seem real now, but I have been on a work farm in Mississippi for the last six months. There's a big plot by some of us to get …"

Monster interrupted. "We gotta go. The truck that brought you here just sped off and I see unmarked police cars pulling in. I think they know you are here. What's the plan?"

Jason's mind was reeling. Grandma Ruby was dead after meeting with some company in Detroit. Rico and Monster had buried her secretly and had been staking out the apartment in hopes he would come back. Now that he was back, the memory of The Farm seemed far away. His reactions were slow because all of a sudden everything seemed to be moving in slow motion.

Rico was loading a gun and frantically saying something to him. Monster shoved Jason into his grandmother's old room and shut the door. Jason heard a loud crash and voices as the apartment door was kicked in.

Monster turned to him and simply said, "Greater love, man. See you later," as he exited the room, closing the door behind him.

A barrage of gunfire erupted on the other side of the door and then silence.

A voice called out, "Jason Warner, we know you are in there. Come out with your hands up." Slowly, Jason opened the door.

He fell to his knees as he looked down into the dead eyes of his childhood friend, Sheldon Storner aka Monster. Monster knew when he left the room he was going to die attempting to protect Jason.

The *greater love* comment was a reference to something they had learned in a fourth grade Vacation Bible School class: *"Greater love hath no man than this, that he would lay down his life for his friends."*

Jason looked around for Rico but didn't see him. His mind was overcome by all that had happened in less than an hour. He staggered. And then all went dark as he felt the momentary pain of the night stick to the back of his head and succumbed to unconsciousness.

Allan circled the block hoping for a sign that Jason had gotten away. The police must have been watching Ruby's apartment. The takedown was strategic and quick. After the sixth time around, Allan parked the truck halfway down the block, close enough to see what was happening, but too far to be detected. He saw one man being put into a squad car and two brought out on stretchers. One person on the stretcher was covered, while another appeared to be injured. Allan experienced sadness he hadn't felt in a long time. He had begun to bond with Jason, but that was over now. Jason would not be returning to The Farm. He slowly pulled the truck away from the curb and started the drive back to rural Mississippi.

***

Jason woke up in a filthy prison cell. His head hurt and his clothes were bloody.

He got up carefully and walked slowly to the glass on the wall. His head was bandaged. He barely recognized himself, though he was still wearing the clothes they had given him at The Farm. He had become so used to moving on a regimented schedule that he panicked because he didn't know what time it was. As the reality of the last few hours sank in, he fell to the floor, partly from physical weakness and partly from the realization that his grandmother and one of his best friends were dead, and he had been arrested. That meant it was either the labor farm until he died or execution.

Jason realized, with some surprise, that none of it mattered. Actually, he thought, he would prefer the execution. The sooner the better. He staggered back to the bed and fell into an exhausted sleep.

Jason realized he was dreaming of a time in the past. His grandmother was young and vibrant and had come to get him from an abusive foster home. She put him in in the back seat of an old car and told him he would be safe now. He remembered feeling warm with the stranger who didn't know about him until right before she came to get him. Because she was a blood relative, and had the means to take care of him, they released him to her. Well, not voluntarily. Only after he told them about the abuse he had suffered at the hands of "those people" did the Family Services Division release him. Jason could smell the scent of her perfume – like flowers, but not too sweet. He watched the back of her head and noticed she was crying.

Through the abandonment and abuse of those responsible for him, Jason had learned to read emotions well and to become silent and invisible. He didn't understand the woman's tears, but found himself silently crying in the backseat without understanding why. Jason was nine years old. He was dreaming of the early years he spent with his grandmother. He could feel the same joy as he dreamed of the times they went to the parks and zoos. He heard the sound of his grandmother's laughter, a light sound like tinkling wind chimes if wind chimes could smile. He loved her laugh. As Jason tried to focus in on his grandmother's laugh, something was bothering him – a noise he didn't recognize.

"Wake up, prisoner. Wake up!"

He was jarred awake by the jab of a stick to his rib cage.

"Wake up. It seems someone has made special provisions for you."

The old men sat around a fire, drinking. Ruby had been one of the first to deed her land to The Farm Network, early when the conversations started about what to do with those young people who had gone astray. She was quiet and dignified, though she didn't have much. It broke her heart to find out she had a son in the system, but the day she found out she went to Child Protective Services and raised holy hell until they found him and gave him to her. Jason had been her whole world, and she gave it all for those like him. The old men viewed the opportunity to help Jason as a way of thanking Ruby. They really wanted him to make it.

They didn't often get discouraged. When Allan came back and told them Jason had been arrested, it wasn't just another thug taken off the street. This time they had let Ruby down. Will and Allan were inconsolable, but Pops, one of the originators of The Farm, reminded them that heartbreaks were part of the job they signed up for.

"Y'all can have one more hour of feeling bad, and then we gotta get ready for the next shift. There are still some here we might be able to help. Plus, we were able to get his friend, so it wasn't a total loss. Drink up and get some sleep. I'll take the watch tonight."

chapter 17: althea

Althea surveyed the new son's living quarters. Compared to the other quarters, the suite of rooms was nice enough to reflect his status as a son, but not so nice that Nicholas would be offended as the eldest son. She knew it would be a delicate dance to integrate a son from the past into her current family and community. Althea didn't doubt that Nicholas had already shared his views on awakening their relative with several in the community. She felt their questioning glances on her daily walks with a combination of embarrassment and anger. Althea knew her mental status was being used as the reason for her decision to awaken their relative. The thought of her son subtly undermining her standing by implying her mental decline, brought tears to her eyes. It was especially painful because in the Community of African Descendants, honor was given to the aged. Nicholas' attitude about her mental state was a throwback to ancient prejudices against elders that was out of step with their lives today. Even those rare elders who experienced mental decline today in the Community were treated honorably and given responsibilities in other communities that affirmed their continuing value.

Althea shook off the sadness as she looked around the new quarters. There was only one thing left to do in here: place the letter. Everyone who was put in cryotechnology received a letter from the person who committed them to the process.

This letter served as an emotional goodbye if the relative wasn't present at the cryofreezing, and included words of hope for a new future. This letter would give some grounding to the person who would awaken in a new place, a new time, and among new relatives.

Althea looked at the handwriting on the envelope, which simply said, *"To My Beloved Grandson."* The writing had the shaky script of a weakened older person. Althea opened the folder and looked at the identification picture with the name, Ruby Warner. Althea held her head to the side, studying the picture. There was hope in those eyes; the same hope Althea saw in her own eyes. There was also the same fatigue she noticed in elders from the time before. They didn't live as long as elders of today, because life was apparently much harder back then. She noticed there was a last name. All of the old last names had been done away with when the Community of African Descendants was established. The original founders of the community wanted to ensure that all vestiges of the trauma from Before were strategically eliminated, including names given to those ancestors by slavers.

Althea said a silent prayer for the woman she would only know through her new son. Across more than a century, they were connected. Althea then asked God to show her how to be a mother to the son she would meet later today. She walked through his quarters, praying for a peaceful transition from before to now, and then gently placed the envelope on the nightstand next to the bed.

chapter 18: jason

"Well, you get to be part of an experiment, inmate," the guard said.

He nodded for Jason to turn around and then placed handcuffs on him. He escorted him out of his cell, through the hallways, and finally, the entry doors to the prison. There was a black van waiting with the emblem, "FFI" in discreet white letters on the side. A man wearing a uniform with the same emblem got out of the passenger side carrying a clipboard.

"J. Warner?", he asked.

The prison guard nodded, signed the clipboard and removed Jason's handcuffs.

The uniformed man took him by the shoulder and helped him step into the back seat of the van.

"Where are you taking me?" Jason asked.

The prison guard walked away as the uniformed man got into the van.

"You are now property of Family Futures Incorporated. You will get more information when we get to our destination. Until then, I suggest you relax and uh...take in the sunshine."

Both the driver and the uniformed man started to laugh. Jason felt a fear he had never felt before. He knew his life was ending and wondered how he felt about that.

chapter 19: rico

Rico felt like an animal. He smelled like one too.

He had woken up in a barracks, where it was as hot as hell must be, wearing a uniform. He tried to remember what happened. They were at Jason's grandma's apartment when the police came. He heard Cookie lock Jason in the room, and the two of them planned to shoot their way out. Through some kind of fluke, he was able to walk out of the apartment – the police had made up their minds that he wasn't worth their time. That's when he heard the barrage of shots and knew the Cookie Monster was dead. He ran down the stairs and straight into another man, tall and dark, who put a handkerchief over his nose and mouth. When he woke up, he was here on some stanky, hot plantation in a barn with at least twelve other men. Someone was yelling to get up, shut up and go eat. *What in the Kunta Kinte was going on?* Rico knew how to follow orders. He got up and followed suit.

chapter 20: jason

The doors to the van opened and Jason was escorted out. There was a man on either side of him, and they walked him into a plain, two-story brick building with no writing or signs on the outside. Inside the building was modern, completely glass and steel. The two men escorted Jason to a receptionist's desk where she appeared to check his name off a list. No one even looked him in the eye or spoke a word to him, they just shuffled him down a long hallway. *An experiment?* he thought to himself. *This feels like a death march.* Jason resigned himself to dying. His grandmother was dead. One of his best friends was dead, and the other was probably in prison or dead too.

The uniformed men escorted Jason through a plain steel door at the end of the hall. It looked like a laboratory of some kind. There was a gurney beside bags and intravenous needles. Jason struggled. *What is going on? I haven't had a trial! Am I being denied due process?*

The uniformed men ignored his struggles as they strapped him to the gurney and placed restraints around his forehead, arms, waist and legs.

"Jason Warner, I wish to read the bequeathment of your grandmother, Ruby: 'I, Ruby Warner, being of sound mind and body, do hereby bequeath all of my resources to Family Futures Incorporated upon signature of this document. Upon the cryofreezing of Jason Warner, I agree that these funds will cover the experimental treatment and storage of one, Jason.

Warner, for up to one hundred sixty years in the future, with the interest paid to our future descendants upon Jason's awakening.'"

Jason's head was spinning. *Grandma Ruby,* he thought. *Why?* He would not cry. He cried as a child in the abusive foster homes. In his last moments alive, neither Grandma Ruby nor anyone else would get another tear from him. This betrayal cut deeper than any pain he had ever felt. This pain was worse than all the abuse, worse than being arrested, and worse than that farm. This pain made death just fine with Jason. He steeled his eyes and looked at the clerk who was reading the papers.

"Do you recognize the signature on this page?"

"Yeah," Jason said. "That is my grandmother's signature." He refused to make eye contact with anyone else in the room.

"Do you acknowledge that you are Jason Warner."

Jason closed his eyes and said, "Yes."

"Let's get started," the clerk said.

Maybe he was more than a clerk. Maybe he was a doctor. Jason didn't care. As the first needle went into his arm, he told himself it didn't matter anymore. That he didn't need tears or love or kindness. But when the second needle went into his arm he felt cold, except for the tear that escaped his closed eyes as darkness closed in all around him.

chapter 21: richard

Richard Ross, the chairman of Farmington Corporation, prepared himself for another day of work. While the corporate name sounded sophisticated, its beginnings were very humble. The business of rehabilitating those often heaced speedily towards destruction is not an easy undertaking.

In the 21st century, as authorities got close to The Farm Network, those in charge formulated an escape plan. Based on laws and how things were going, they knew there would always be a need for an organization that protected and rehabilitated those from the community who had gone astray. Their escape plan included identifying someone who was currently part of The Farm Network, but possessed extreme leadership potential. Once identified that individual would go under rigorous training, be given an assumed name with a family that had signed up for FFI, and just before the farm network was shut down, that leader would be put into cryosleep. The old men decided none of them would be fit for the future; they needed to identify one of the trainees and trust him to carry their vision forward.

Richard Ross was that important figure. Mr. Henry was one of the leaders in The Farm Network, and after spending years being trained under him, Richard felt like family. Mr. Henry had agreed to take Richard in as one of their own, but Richard had to agree to be the seed for The Farm Network's future.

Richard missed the rules and norms of the past. In the past, selling drugs was criminal. In this time, on the outside, it was just another industry. There were still people who didn't sell or participate in the drug industry, but industry is how it was known. The human costs were still the same- death from overdose, financial poverty, family loss, and addiction. The stupid territorial battles had gotten worse too. Just because drug dealing was legal, didn't mean it wasn't pricey for the individuals and communities involved.

Outside the activities of Farmington Corporation, Richard lived a solitary life. The men and women who came through their doors knew that the chairman was not one to be toyed with. His tough precision in dealing with anyone who dared cross him or violate the rules of Farmington Corporation was infamous. When Farmington residents signed over their rights to the corporation, they were investing in a new life. They either learned to live a new way or died trying.

Farmington Corporation wasn't entirely altruistic, though. In order to do the work, Farmington, and by extension, Richard, needed to form some partnerships. These partnerships didn't always align with the mission of helping others to live better more productive lives, but the money from the partnerships did. For instance, there was an elder inside the Commune of African Descendants who had made considerable investments to buy influence as a shadow shareholder in Farmington.

chapter 22: jason (awakening)

There were needles sticking him all over his body. Jason faded in and out as he tried to process the sting of the needles and the muffled voices that seemed to be coming from far away. He blinked, realizing that he had been asleep and tried to clear his head by shaking it. Focusing, Jason looked at the people standing around his bed.

There was a doctor or someone with scme kind of clipboard. He was speaking numbers into it. He looked around at a nurse who was monitoring his pulse. There was an old lady -

"Grandma?"

He winced as he remembered his grandmother was dead. A technician came in and started removing wires from his fingers, neck, arms and legs. Jason watched, still trying to make sense of what happened. The last thing he remembered was getting a shot and falling asleep.

Fear registered in Jason's eyes as he remembered the words:"You get to be part of an experiment." Jason began struggling against the restraints on his arms.

Althea quickly ran to his side and placed a comforting hand on his arm. "I know you don't understand, but you're going to be just fine. I'm so glad you're here. My name is Althea, and you are part of my family now."

Her voice sounded old and wise, yet young and lilting at the same time. He looked in her eyes, attempting to place how he might know her. She looked like someone he might have known, but he didn't know any Althea.

"If you can trust me," Althea continued, "I will have them remove the restraints. It's ok," she smiled kindly. "When you're ready, we'll come back and take you home."

Jason nodded.

"The doctors have to run a few more tests, and then we will be back to collect you." Seeing his fear start to rise again, Althea gently kissed the young man on his forehead. "See you in a little while."

Jason watched her leave and then looked to the doctor. "What happened to me?"

chapter 23: the farm

Allan grudgingly thought Rico could be the replacement for the plans they originally had for Jason at The Farm. The "Pretty Boy," as they nicknamed him, had a lot more grit than the leaders initially gave him credit for. He was obviously a good soldier in whatever criminal organization he had been part of, but there was a mental toughness that only those familiar with leading could identify. Rico literally talked to no one at meals, and only as needed for work. Clearly, he was watching, perhaps looking for an opportunity to get away. Allan and the group agreed to watch Rico's demeanor for another week before starting conversations with him.

Rico had been on The Farm three months before he was approached by one of the leaders. He felt their eyes on him as he went about the labor on the farm. Rico understood structure and pecking order when he saw it, and he knew how to keep his head down and eyes open until he figured out what was going on. Allan was especially hard on Rico, always ordering him to do extra to see how he would react. Rico knew that game too; he had initiated new recruits in Jason's organization that way. Those who couldn't handle the pressure cracked early and were eliminated from any positions of responsibility. Those who handled the rough parts well could be trusted with the responsibilities of leading.

Rico could handle rough. When some of the older guys came to him after work last week, he was suspicious. They had done nothing but ride him since he had been at The Farm. Now he was being asked to eat with them. He wondered what their angle was.

Allan started. "Your being here wasn't planned. You may have learned that all the men here were requisitioned by a family member. Look around."

Rico looked out the large window at the dozens of men who were eating in a makeshift cafeteria.

"Some relative called us here at The Farm and made arrangements to save these men from certain arrest or death. The mothers, fathers, grandparents, aunts or uncles, spent their last dollars so the men you see here could be taught a different way of living. We have some moderate success. Only about 20% of the men you see will return to the streets. The rest of them will learn a trade either here or on one of the other farms and start a new life. The biggest change, though, happens right here," Allan said pointing to his head. "That's why life here is so hard at first."

Rico waited for Allan to get to the point as he looked around the table at the other men whose names were Will, Rufus and Henry.

Henry spoke up. "You didn't get here the way the other men did. You are here in Jason's place. Jason's grandmother arranged for him to be here because his arrest was imminent." Henry paused, "She knew the law was coming for him. You all think you're so slick that you can't get caught, but there's always someone in your organization who will give names in exchange for the appearance of a little more freedom.

Your crew had been sold out and it was a matter of time before you all were taken down. Because we hadn't heard from Ruby, we agreed to let Jason go check on her. It appears all hell broke loose, and Jason was taken anyway. We know you've lost two friends, but those losses don't have to be for nothing."

Rico looked composed on the outside but felt like he was going to be sick. First, he just learned that this is where Jason had been the whole time they were looking for him.

"I need to use the restroom," Rico said.

Allan nodded towards the hallway.

As he walked towards the bathroom, Rico could hear the men mumbling.

One of them said, "It might be too soon. We should have waited another week."

He could make out Allan's voice disagreeing, "We need to get started. We don't have a whole lot of time."

Rico slowed down to hear more of the conversation.

chapter 24: jason

The doctor calmly explained to Jason that he had been in cryosleep for 200 years, and that the decision was made by his family to wake him up rather than terminate him.

Jason was angry and numb.

"What family?" his voice thundered. "The only living relative I had was my grandmother and she is dead!"

Jason and the doctor stared at each other for what seemed like hours.

Finally, the doctor resumed his explanation. "Yes, we see that your grandmother died a while ago. But you have relatives here in this time who are responsible for you now."

"What year is this?" Jason asked.

"Today is June 16, 2200," the doctor responded. "Your vitals are within the normal range and there are no underlying conditions. You are free to go. I will have the nurse send in your relative." The doctor turned and unceremoniously left the room.

Althea came back into the room. She did resemble Grandma Ruby, if Grandma had been healthy, unworried and rich.

"I know you have a lot of questions. I am here for you, but I respect that you will need time to process all of this. There are some things at home that will help you, I think. Are you ready to go home now?

Althea's face and voice were comforting, and her voice was tentative when she said "home." Where else would he go?

As Jason and Althea left the medical center, he felt like a child in a science fiction playground. There were flying cars, they called them conveyances, and moving walkways everywhere. Althea took him by the arm and steered him into a conveyance at the curb. Inside was a calming smell and soothing temperature. He had no words. His senses were overwhelmed as he tried to fathom where he was and where he had been. Jason saw Althea out of the corner of his eye looking at him with concern.

Althea had her own sets of concerns. She had never awakened a sleeping relative before- this was a first for their family. She had read in the information that those awakened were often disoriented for days and even weeks as they tried to reconcile the past with a brand new present. She had directed the conveyance to take the longer, more scenic route to their home. She hoped this would give Jason extra time to process. The ride home was much quieter than she expected.

When the conveyance stopped in front of the commune there was a short pause as the beautiful ivy gates slowly swung open. The scene before him was breathtaking. There were no streets, but pleasant walking ways, ponds, and homes that seemed to blend in with the sky, the water and the greenery. Jason followed Althea silently. In the distance he heard the laughter of children, and all around there was a feeling of calm, but more than that. Was it peace?

The feeling was foreign to Jason, but it permeated the entire environment. The feeling made him feel even more like a stranger.

Althea said quietly, "Follow me this way to your quarters. I have tried to make it comfortable for you with some items that are familiar."

She opened the door to a room with windows that caught some of the sunset. The colors were calming, lots of grays and shades of blue. Even though the room was tasteful, it looked as if it was waiting for a personality to move in. On the table to the right was an envelope, and on the left, a picture of Grandma Ruby.

Althea spoke quietly, "Would you like to have something to eat now with me, or would you prefer to eat alone today?"

"I am hungry," Jason said. "But may I have a few minutes to collect myself? I feel like I'm spinning, and I just need to stop for a moment."

Althea nodded. "I'm right next door. My door will be open, and I will wait for you as long as you need." She quietly closed Jason's door and left the room.

Jason watched the door close and looked around the room. It was very nice, nicer than anything he had before. It was afternoon and the eastern facing room gave him a breathtaking view of evening shadows. He walked over to the balcony and looked out. There were children and elders in a circle on the lawn practicing recitations. He thought of his grandmother and turned away as a lone tear ran down his cheek. On the nightstand were two pictures of them.

The first was taken when he was about nine, just after she rescued him from the system. His eyes looked sad and scared. He closed his eyes as the memory of that day came rushing back. He hadn't known if he could trust this old woman who had come out of nowhere. The first night in her apartment, they both cried as she made up the sofa sleeper. She kept saying, "I didn't know about you. I never would have left you. I'm so sorry." He took a deep breath as he remembered that first long, warm hug.

The second picture on the nightstand was of him and Grandma Ruby after he became an adult. He had taken her out to a fancy dinner for her birthday. He remembered how impressed and happy she was that day. The waiter took a picture of them, and she had it framed.

"Grandma Ruby, what did you do?" Jason whispered as his voice broke. He looked at the envelope on the nightstand, took a breath and opened it.

Dear Jason,

The first thing I want to tell you is that I'm sorry. I'm sorry that I won't get to see you again. I know that now. Believe it or not, everything I did, I did to protect you. It was me who had you picked up by the people from The Farm. I know what you do. You sell drugs. It was only a matter of time before the police came for you and did God knows what. I can't take a chance on losing you again. Jason, you are all I got.

The second thing I want to tell you is that I made a deal with this FFI company, to save a place for your future. If for some reason you still get picked up, you are property of FFI, and the police can't hurt you. I don't have much, but I have just enough. If our family goes on, you will have a shot in the future. Maybe things will be better for us then, they certainly can't get much worse.

The last thing I want to say is that I love you. You are my heart, Jason. I would have given my life for you a thousand times over if I could. I'm so sorry for the pain you suffered before I knew about you. I'm also sorry for the pain you will feel when you wake up one day in a different place and time. Please take this chance and be the man I know you can be. You are a leader. You made a lonely old woman's last days joyful and meaningful. Take my gift to you and live.

I'll love you forever,
Grandma Ruby

So, Grandma Ruby was planning while Jason thought he was fooling her. He read the letter three times, each time crying more than the last. Feeling like a used dishrag, hunger started to rumble in Jason's stomach. He went into his bathroom and splashed water on his face. Then he got up and went to find Althea.

chapter 25: the farm

"We have reason to believe The Farm has come under scrutiny by the authorities," Allan spoke. "The Farm Network runs throughout the south. Black families have owned land in the South since the end of slavery, much of it just sitting. When the elders saw what was happening in society, how slavery was being reinstituted through the prison system, they began to talk. For the last ten years, we have been under the radar, grabbing boys at risk for arrest or murder, teaching trades, and returning men to communities to start new lives. The land was given by the elders who owned it, but The Farm is self-sustaining. We grow what we eat, we build where we live, and we put all our hope in what we do here for the future."

"Why are you telling me this?" Rico asked.

Henry angrily replied, "Because some of the men from town who don't know what we're doing are stirring up trouble. One of our contacts in the local sheriff's office says these crackers are calling for an investigation into the farms and why they never hear about openings for jobs or trade programs."

Henry got up pacing angrily. "We have been building something to better our men, our families, our communities for the last ten years. We've done good work!" he shouted. "But some of these people want to shut us down, use old laws to take back land and destroy everything we've built because they can't get their hands on it."

Henry's anger was smoldering.

"What Henry is saying is that we need a backup plan – a failsafe in case we're shut down suddenly," Allan stood up. "We are planning some things that we can't tell everyone, but we want you to be part of the plan. This means, you must commit to be part of The Farm for the very, very long haul," Allan said solemnly.

Rufus looked at Henry and Allan, "Tell him the terms and let him think about it. If he's not in, it doesn't make sense to tell him anymore, and we can take him back to the city and leave him on his own. For all we know, he could still be looking for a way out of here anyway."

Rufus turned to look at Rico.

Rico didn't say a word or look away from his glance. For a few tense moments the two men stared at each other.

Breaking the tension, Allan said, "The deal is you commit to do what it takes to make sure The Farm continues as long as there are young men who can be picked up, imprisoned without trial or misused by the system, or we drop you off where we found you and let you take your chances. The choice is yours."

the future
chapter 26: jason

Althea and Jason walked around the commune after dinner. Today was intentionally just between them, no other family members were present as she introduced Jason to his new life. Dinner had been a mixture of the familiar and brand new. The tastes and smells of the food he ate were inviting and clean. No one looked at him during dinner or attempted to engage him. The commune had a practice to *respect the journey* of those who had awakened. The time to travel mentally, emotionally and spiritually to a world hundreds of years from your last memory was not the same for everyone. The commune recognized that while the body was here, the soul had to catch up.

Jason asked, "What is this place? How far are we from where I lived?"

Althea smiled. "This place didn't exist in your before. Through the agreements made with FFI, the families decided to use the riches received to negotiate, fight for and build a new place. It wasn't easy; the governments were dealing with people of color from a place of domination. With the fight and the world courts on our side, we were able to create a new society – a province might be a way for you to understand it. This new place would nourish and protect our children by teaching them values that had been lost through hundreds of years of oppression and racism. This place would celebrate families from birth to the grave by employing the principles of honor and respect.

73

This place would respect the God who made all by nourishing the earth and caring for it as we care for each other. This place didn't exist before. Because of people like your grandmother, we were able to make The Commune of African Descendants a reality. We are a community of families, all beginning with a brave person from your time, who through the FFI experiments, sent resources through time. The resources were not just money, though. I pray that those who come to us from before will bring the best of those family members with them. You, Jason, connect us to our past."

chapter 27: rico

Rico knew this was a real crossroads. He lay in the barracks, not sleeping all night. He had become accustomed to the routine of waking up early, hard work, eating and sleeping. He had been a street soldier for more than ten years. These people knew nothing about the people he had murdered, or the random remorse that sometimes came out of nowhere. In spite of how easy he made it look, Rico's calm killing always carried emotional and spiritual backlash. He was a physically attractive man who had never had a real girlfriend or a serious relationship. The idea of exposing his heart was dangerous; something ugly could leak out and hurt someone bad. Rather than believe in his value to creation, Rico chose to sidestep any discussions about purpose, the future, or contributing to someone else's story. In his mind, his story would end with a bullet —alone.

Strange, though, because he came from a family of Believers. REAL BELIEVERS. He was the little boy who had brought Jason and Monster to Vacation Bible School. Sometimes he caught a mental picture of the wide-eyed, joyful boy that he was back then; but those pictures came far less frequently than they once had. He smiled wryly. *Drowned out by all the blood he had directly encountered,* he thought, starting with his mother.

People said Rico got his good looks from his mother. She was a beautiful mix of Chicago cool and Puerto Rican hot.

If he stopped, he could still see her laughing and dancing in the family's South Side apartment. His father was not home as often after he lost his job. He told Rico that he was starting his own side hustle to take care of their family and might be away longer than he liked. Daddy always came home, though. But things had changed. His mother didn't laugh as much as she used to, though her face always lit up when Rico came into the room. He heard his parents arguing after they thought he was asleep. Before losing his job, their family had been ideal – one of the few on the block with both parents. Before they went to church every Sunday, where all of Rico's best friends were. Now Daddy was gone, sometimes for days at a time, and Mom spent more time praying and less time laughing.

Rico shuddered as the memory of that day came back. He had not thought about it in years. The day everything changed had been a normal day. Rico and some friends had stopped by the candy store on the way home from school. They walked together, each saying goodbye as they arrived at their home. Rico's building was at the end of the block, so he was always the last of his friends to get home. As he arrived, he saw two men hastily running from the building. He stopped to let them by. *The people on the first floor had a lot of company,* he thought. He watched them leave, waiting until they were a safe distance in case they came back. Walking up the stairs he found the outside door open. He closed it tight like his mom always taught him to do, to keep himself safe.

Walking up the stairs to his family's apartment, he found their door open too. A feeling, something he had never felt, made him afraid.

Walking into the living room, he noticed his father's shoes were in the wrong place, and his father's legs and feet were still in them. His mind started taking pictures: the shoes facing upward, attached to Daddy's pants. Daddy looking straight ahead with an expression like he was daydreaming. A hole on the side of Daddy's head with blood trickling out.

Rico shook his head, trying to make sense of what he was seeing. Why was Daddy laying here daydreaming?

"Daddy," he said tentatively.

His father didn't respond. He remembered that second shake of his head - that's when the boy knew something was very wrong.

Mama. He had to find Mama.

Rico ran to the kitchen, and to the back of the house to his parents' bedroom. He heard the heavy breathing on the side of the bed. Running, he saw his mother, but she looked sick. Something was wrong. There was blood everywhere.

She whispered his name, "Rico, I'm sorry. Come here," she beckoned.

Rico knelt beside her and looked in her eyes.

"I love you, baby." She tried to hug him, and that's when Rico started to cry. He cried until day turned to night, and day again.

And he never cried again.

Oddly, tonight lying in bed considering the offer the men made him, he felt like crying. Rico had lost Jason and Monster, who had become the only family he knew. A series of abusive foster homes had hardened him and exposed him to the worst in humanity. He didn't talk about it, didn't even think about it – but the emotional distance had served him well. These men were asking for something else though. They wanted him to commit to a plan beyond what any of them could see or imagine.

the future
chapter 28: nicholas

Nicholas met Elder Benjamin outside of the Commune. While Nicholas appeared to disdain life outside the Commune of African Descendants, he had spent a considerable amount of time Outside. Outside of the commune, life was very different. Elder Benjamin had introduced Nicholas to the outside when he was much younger, in his late teens. The elder was smart enough to know when a teenage boy became adventurous. Since introducing young Nicholas to the outside, Nicholas and Benjamin met regularly beyond the safety and discretion of the commune. This place, where the food was greasy, the staff grubby, and the conversation illicit, was a favorite of both Nicholas and Elder Benjamin.

"So," Elder Benjamin said, "I understand your mother has awakened a relative. Have you considered what that means for your position as potential chief elder?"

Nicholas attempted to measure his words.

"Speak freely," Benjamin said.

"I'm angry," Nicholas replied. "I voiced my truth to my mother about how I believe a sleeper would affect our community, but she didn't hear me. We have been at odds on major issues for a few years now. I believe it's her intent to give this sleeper the same rights I have. Never has there been a sleeper who was put in position to be chief elder of a tribe. I am angry, and I feel overlooked by my own mother."

"Do you believe she is losing her mental faculties," Benjamin asked. "Think carefully before you answer: there are some consequences to your tribe if she is losing her mental faculties and is unmarried. You will have to prove that in a court of those from your tribe, and have that choice ratified by the elders of the other tribes. Your mother is among the most influential elders in the commune. Taking her on and losing would put you in a very negative position and could actually open the way for the sleeper to take your place as your mother's heir."

"What should I do?", Nicholas asked.

"The way I see it, you have three options to consider, but to do so would mean you need resources –*significant resources.*" Elder Benjamin watched Nicholas to see if he clearly understood the meaning of *resources*.

Nicholas knew what Elder Benjamin meant. Unlike many in the commune, Nicholas knew the source of the older man's influence, both within and outside the Commune. Elder Benjamin had been grooming young Nicholas when he first decided to pursue Althea decades ago. While Althea had rejected his advances, Benjamin still believed Nicholas would be beneficial in his pursuit of the Chief Elder position. Benjamin had introduced Nicholas to the science of investing in the illicit trades Outside and creating influence among those citizens. Outside the Commune, for instance, the sale and use of drugs was no longer illegal – expensive, but now legal. Food, medicine and merchandise from the Commune commanded a high price in the illicit market.

This merchandise, which included Commune created medicines, could be traded for just about anything. Those from the Commune who were responsible for trade, only negotiated with societies that adhered to the same values of humanity and care for the earth. However, Benjamin had found plenty of others who cared nothing of those values, but who were willing to pay a higher price for the same trade. Benjamin was known outside The Commune as the source for procuring Commune items on the black market. His markups on merchandise, medicine, and food were five times what legitimate trade partners paid. Bennie, as he was known Outside, and Elder Benjamin, were wealthy men, both inside the Commune and Outside.

Nicholas was only a small trading partner Outside. He dealt with the same three people, and had a much smaller financial footprint than Benjamin, but he understood the ecosystem that made one wealthy Outside could make one influential in the Commune. Though it wasn't common knowledge, Benjamin had shared which elders could be influenced by the rotten fruit of mammon. Nicholas was becoming less surprised. It seems his mother and a few others were among the few who couldn't be lured off their "porches of principle," as Benjamin called it. Nicholas could still hear his mother's words from his childhood: "If we don't maintain our light, we will descend into the darkness of Before." He shook off the thought and turned his attention back to Elder Benjamin.

"What are my three options?", Nicholas asked.

chapter 29: rico

Rico had to break with everyone he knew. *Not a problem,* he thought. Jason and Monster were gone. None of his foster "families" had anything to do with him after his first arrest. Nope, leaving past relationships wouldn't be a problem. Next, he had to commit to the plan no matter what happened. This meant as part of the internal structure he ran the same risk of death or worse as the old men. Hmmm. That wasn't a problem either; after all, he ran those risks on the street every day. Next, he needed to agree to be The Farm's future guinea pig. That was the scary part.

The talk about an incoming raid and arrest was increasing, and Henry told Rico he needed to decide today or go back to the streets. Rico had no one and nothing to go back to. The decision to stay with The Farm was easy. The only thing to leave behind was everything Rico knew.

the future: nicholas

Nicholas' ideas of increasing his footprint Outside would allow him to buy the support of some elders to have his mother declared incompetent, though not enough. He could also directly take on his mother for the role of Chief Elder without declaring her incompetent – just irrelevant.

Lastly, he could destroy Althea's credibility with the Commune by peddling influence on the outside in a way that would point back to her. All three strategies were risky.

Benjamin said, "Well, let me help you. I'm going to introduce you to the head of The Farmington Corporation, one of our partners on the Outside."

chapter 30: checkmate (the farm)

Three words flashed through The Farm Network's cell system at the same time: **"Implement Failsafe. Go."** This wasn't a drill. The national organization known as The Farm had one hour to implement its doomsday plan. Henry put Rico in the back of the truck and left the south for Detroit. By the time the raids started, they would be out of Mississippi. Residents of other Farms did the same. One designated driver and one "seed" left each location. The men left on The Farm were called together by location and told of the impending raid. They were given a choice: leave now for wherever you want to go or stay and fight. Overall, 80% of The Farm's residents left.

The first raid happened at the North Carolina farm. The text came back over the network: "Raiders not cops. Cops overseeing. Going dark. See you on the other side." Barry, in North Carolina, bashed his phone, destroying it with a hammer and picked up his rifles. There were fifteen of them there and they would hold off these crackers for as long as they could. One by one, each farm fell violently with 100% casualties among those who stayed and fought. The men who left were scattered. Many returned to their communities, and were promptly arrested and imprisoned without trial. Others simply vanished. The land was confiscated from its original owners because of the illegal activities they were accused of housing.

The machinery and crops mysteriously disappeared before the land was eventually burned. The entire process of desecrating The Farm Network took two weeks. More than 6,000 men were killed as government sponsored terrorists violently destroyed the land and legacies of thousands of families.

henry

The old man walked off the elevator into the nicely modern offices of FFI. "I have papers on file here for one of my relatives. Is this where I bring him before he's arrested?" The receptionist nodded, not speaking. The designated seed from their farm came up behind him and hugged the old man. Henry refused to meet his eyes. "You go on now. You've been a good son." Henry turned and never looked back as he walked out the door and disappeared into the crowded city. "The Seed" understood his assignment. He followed the technician through the glass doors.

chapter 31: the new son

In his first week here, Jason had been isolated with Althea as she helped him understand the Commune of African Descendants. It was interesting being called "my son," by Althea. He didn't recall ever being anyone's son, and he wasn't sure he liked it. Understanding that until his naming ceremony, he would be referred to in these terms, was screwing with his sense of identity. And his sense of identity was already questionable. The only thing he recognized about himself was his face. Everything that made him "Jason" was gone: his grandmother, his home, his friends, his life. Walking through the Commune and being greeted as "my son" by people he didn't know was both comforting and unnerving. It was comforting to feel like he was accepted and belonged to those within the Commune. It was unnerving because he had done nothing to earn the acceptance, so he felt the sense of belonging could be rescinded as easily as it had been offered.

Apparently, Jason also had a brother that he would meet today. One thing that had followed him into this time was his instincts about people. He discerned that the reason he hadn't met this brother already was because of some issue his brother had with him.

Althea stood and extended her arms to Nicholas. Jason noted that Nicholas' return hug did not express the same warmth of his mother's hug.

Nicholas turned to face Jason. "My brother," he said coldly.

"Nicholas," Jason responded. Jason's instincts had been right; his brother had a problem with him. Jason assumed it was because of the potential shared family responsibility that Althea mentioned. Whatever Nicholas' issue was with him, it wouldn't be solved by a custom of acceptance. Jason knew at some point he and Nicholas were going to have it out, but in this time and place he didn't know what that would look like.

Althea broke the awkward silence between the two men. "Let's have the evening meal together. We can talk and get to know each other better."

That first dinner was the beginning of a series of awkward meals and family discussions. One by one, Jason was introduced to the elders and their families under Althea's leadership. For the most part, the families were warm and welcoming, but distant as they waited to see how "the new son" would acclimate to the Commune. They had all read about the time Jason had lived in, and could surmise about the challenges he would face as he became a new person in a new time. This commune-wide familiarity with the times past was required when a son was awakened. Understanding his time would allow the Village to provide greater intellectual and emotional support.

Salty brother aside, Jason was beginning to feel relaxed and at peace. He found enjoyment in the feel of the sun, and in studying how the Commune provided food and medicine to the residents.

Most disease had been eliminated through the combination of healthy food without preservatives, medicines that grew from the ground and careful attention to mental and emotional well-being. Most of the foods Jason knew from before could not be found here. He was learning to identify different tastes and like new foods. Though not completely vegetarian, proteins were fish and plant based, with fowl at different times of the year.

Jason remembered his grandmother and how she would have benefitted from the knowledge that was common in the Commune. Grandma Ruby would have surely lived longer because of both the food and medicine. The quality of her later years would have been better as well. He could picture her in the Community of Elders and Children, singing songs and passing along knowledge. He stopped and looked away from the microscope as he let the memory of her wash over him.

"My brother, are you well?" The song-like voice of Hester shook Jason out of his daydream.

Hester was Jason's guide in the Community of Life and Science. This community was responsible for researching conditions that had traditionally afflicted people of African Descent and identifying solutions. The community's principle was, "Study science in the context of life." Their team studied everything from the effects of diet on life, to the effects of broken families on health. The Community of Life and Science was responsible for shaping the Commune's approach to well-being.

Jason shook himself again. "I was thinking of my grandmother, and how having this information would have helped her live longer."

Hester admired the new son. He didn't talk much, but it was obvious he had high intellectual curiosity. That kind of curiosity always spoke to a high level of intelligence. He also wasn't hard to look at.

"I'm sorry," Hester responded. "That must be hard for you to think about. It seems to me, though," Hester continued, "that your grandmother knew you had the ability to make life better for others. Otherwise, why would she have gone to the expense of sending you here? She would be proud of you, My Brother."

Hester looked away quickly so the new son wouldn't see her admiring glance.

Jason caught glimpses of Hester when she wasn't looking. She was beautiful and smart. In his time, he had limited involvement with women and no serious ones. It didn't fit with his lifestyle and his priority of taking care of his grandmother. But in this time, relationships were different. There were no casual relationships in the Commune. Romantic relationships required both time and the approval of family members. Relationships were looked at from the perspective of the entire Commune. The joining of a couple was not just about themselves, but about the growth and protection of the Commune's way of life.

Besides, Jason had to figure out his place in this time. Relationships would have to wait. Just as he turned back to the microscope, he caught a glimpse of Althea outside of the window taking her mid-afternoon stroll. He decided to join her.

Nicholas watched as Jason became part of the Commune. While there were still small pockets of resistance to the awakenings, the new son seemed to be winning them over. The new son had developed a particular interest in the Community of Life and Science. He was spending much of his time learning about the medicines and gardens in the Commune. He appeared to have a natural aptitude for which seeds produced the best harvest. Nicholas felt the beginning of an idea forming. A way to discredit Althea as a leader, and to rid the Commune of the sleeper at the same time.

His mother's voice interrupted his thoughts.

"Nicholas," Althea inquired, "Will you walk with me in the gardens? We haven't talked, just the two of us, since the new son joined us."

Nicholas wanted to scream, "NO! I don't want to walk or talk with you. I want you to leave me alone and let me become Chief Elder." Instead, he shook himself and said softly, "Of course, Mother. I would like that."

chapter 33: richard

The irony of running the Farmington Corporation wasn't lost on Richard. He was here because a group of old men from the past wanted to see young men freed from the necessities of a life of crime. Today the penalties weren't legal, they were economic. In this time the resources to fund Farmington's programs came in large part from the same illicit trade that those old men had tried to shut down. Richard decided he would be neutral, which wasn't hard for him at all.

He had to be neutral for the sake of Farmington Corporation, but that didn't eliminate the questions he had. Richard had dealt with people at all levels, from those highly placed in the crackerjack government that still ran some states, to the sovereign states and provinces, and down to the common street dealers. Corruption at any of those levels never made him blink. What felt weird, though, was the uneasy partnership he held with the man from the Commune of African Descendants. This man always set off a loud gong inside Richard that was decidedly not neutral.

Richard shook it off. Business was business, and the meeting he had with Bennie and some new guy was important. The medicines and pure food from the Commune commanded a high price, and those margins alone kept Farmington comfortably in the black.

Because of the margins on products from the Commune, Farmington could afford to keep a supply of food and medicine to feed those families who were trying to start over. Their health was often poor because of the high supply of drugs and the low availability of food and medicine. He reminded himself of the help Farmington was able to provide because of "shadow man" as he called Bennie to himself. Yes, like it or not, Richard would have to keep meeting with the shadow influencer from The Commune.

Some mornings Richard joined the crew doing manual labor in Farmington's factory. These were the mornings he needed physical work to take his mind off the questions he had since being awakened in this strangely familiar time. Today was one of those mornings. He stood and checked his attire in the mirror before meeting the leader from the Commune.

The conference area of Farmington Corporation had none of the grittiness evident in the factory or operations area. Here, there was modern equipment and furnishings. The receptionist had provided refreshments to Bennie and the new person he brought with him.

Richard eyed him suspiciously. "Good afternoon, Bennie. Who is your associate?"

"This is Nicholas," Bennie replied. "I have been grooming him to eventually take my place as your contact with the Commune. As we seek out new partnerships for the Commune, I thought it would be good to introduce you to other associates that I work with."

There was that gong again, Richard thought. "Great," he said. "What are you offering for sale today?"

Bennie started, "Before we talk about sales, I want to start by renegotiating the wholesale price of the cancer-killing formulas. We have been making a small amount on those sales, but the products sell for five times what we sell them to you for. Surely you can afford a 25% increase in the wholesale costs of such a valuable product."

Richard rubbed the left side of his temple. "Whether or not we can afford the product is not the issue. We have an arrangement that is mutually beneficial. Why the increase?"

Bennie looked at Nicholas. "I must bring on help to manage the work outside the Commune, and that help has to be compensated. I know that your work involves helping those who are starting over, so I believe you can appreciate the…" Bennie paused, clearing his throat, "cost of expansion."

Both men stared at each other for an uncomfortable amount of time.

Nicholas broke the silence. "My mother is in preparation to leave her position as Chief Elder of our clan. That position is rightfully mine, and for the sake of a good relationship I would be happy to enhance the terms of our relationship once she has moved on. I assure you, uh," Nicholas paused, "Richard, I assure you that any inconvenience now will be more than made up later."

Richard looked from Bennie to Nicholas. If it were possible, Nicholas set off a bigger gong than Bennie.

"Who will I be dealing with?" Richard asked.

Nicholas looked at Bennie. "I have someone in mind who would be perfect for this. Give me a few weeks to get him ready and make sure I can trust him."

"Now, can we agree in principle on the wholesale pricing of the cancer killing formulas?"

Richard nodded, albeit reluctantly.

Yes, Nicholas thought. *This is the plan that would get rid of both of his family problems.*

chapter 34: althea

Althea woke up and realized she was crying. Her dreams always either warned or reassured her about any direction she was contemplating. This was something different. She couldn't remember the entire dream, only tears and seeing her son. *Ok, Althea, breathe,* she thought. Getting up slowly, she looked to the night sky outside her window. Had she made a mistake awakening the new sor? Was the sense of betrayal she felt in the dream a result of her decision? Standing, Althea lifted her hands to the sky in a deep body stretch and breathed in deeply. As her emotions subsided, she remembered the thought and prayer that led to her decision to awaken the new son. Althea never made decisions lightly, nor did she ruminate excessively over them. She moved decisively and rarely questioned her actions. This dream made her, for a few moments, wonder if she had done the right thing.

She took a deep breath as she finished her stretching routine. Her head was clearer as she went to make a cup of dandelion coffee. She loved this quiet time before family spiritual gathering. *Yes,* she decided. She had made the right decision in waking the sleeping son. She had watched his fascination with growing things and how they related to life in the Commune. Althea realized he was forming insights not just on how aspects of Commune life were related, but what their needs would be in the future.

Hester was the beloved niece of Elder Benjamin. Elder Benjamin had no daughters, only sons who had followed him into the financial work of the Commune. Hester's mother, Laura, was Elder Benjamin's sister-in-law. Laura was married to Benjamin's older brother, Raphael, before he was moved to the Commune of Transition. Benjamin and Raphael's family had come from a long line of businesspeople – those who were able to capitalize on opportunities early enough to get rich. Historically, the financiers who benefitted from cryosleep were guilty of financial crimes. During monthly family celebrations, the history around their families always indicated an intelligence, legal or not, that created wealth for themselves.

On her mother's side, Hester's heritage produced a different kind of intelligence. Hester had loved growing things since she was a child. When family histories were told at monthly celebrations, she was always fascinated by the distant relative, Anatsui, who had worked for the drug-producing conglomerates of the past.

Anatsui had researched and discovered ways of curing the deadliest diseases and was warned against sharing what he learned. When he persisted in his research and findings, he was terminated from his life's work without adequate time to gather his research.

After leaving the employ of the pharmaceutical industry, he was discredited and accused of violating ethics. He was never allowed to work in the drug producing segment again. He lost everything and ended up living among the poorest of those from the time before. Interestingly, however, while living among those who could not afford wellness care, Anatsui created cures from the earth that resulted in an almost non-existent death rate among them. He took on the name, Dr. Anatsui, after the Ghanian artist known for creating art out of discarded things, and to hide from his former employers. Anatsui's cures were made from what he found in the ground. Dr. Anatsui taught what he knew to his children and lived anonymously with his family in a tent on the streets until the day he was found dead with a needle of some substance in his arm.

Anatsui knew the effects both legal and illegal drugs had on society. Despite his deep depression after losing everything, he never resorted to drug use. The whispers around the tent city where Dr. Anatsui and his family lived were that important looking men had been seen lurking around the tents, watching.

Anatsui still had one trick left, though. Before losing his life's work, he had invested in FFI. When the police came looking for his son to imprison him on trumped up charges, they discovered he was property of FFI. Nathan Anatsui was among the first awakened in the future. Awakened with him was the knowledge he had learned from his father. Hester's mother was a descendant of Anatsui and his son Nathan.

Hester inherited the curiosity and intellectual ability to continue the tradition of healing by using what was found in the earth.

In the pursuit of healing, Hester was different from her uncle and cousins, who concerned themselves with the financial independence of the Commune. Hester's father was Elder Benjamin's older brother and neither had much knowledge of their ancestors. He only knew that some were involved in the banking industry from before. Many in that industry had seen the opportunity in FFI, and during the financial crash of 2030, had sent a few members ahead into the future.

Hester stretched her arms and neck and let her mind drift to her family. She had been peering through the microscope at different strains from the plants they had crossbred. The next step was to extract the oils from the new strains and test them. She looked over at the new brother. He was intelligent, curious, and pleasant in appearance. She also sensed a desire to belong and to prove himself. Having been born into this time and Commune,Hester had never experienced a sense of unbelonging. All the sleepers who had been awakened seemed to experience this, and in every previous case it led to them being exiled from the Commune. She hoped the new brother would be the exception. The Commune could benefit from his intelligence and desire to contribute. Hester stretched again and looked at her timepiece. She was meeting her mother for their afternoon walk today, and she didn't want to be late.

Hester's mother, Laura, was a beloved figure in the Justice Forward Circle. As a young woman she had encountered Elder Raphael, Benjamin's brother, as they refined the standards to accommodate the sleepers. The work of the JFC was to ensure that those in the Commune never experienced the effects of caste-based systems that favored one group over another. The eight members of the Circle carried the history and the pain of previous generations. All tribes agreed, as part of their existence in the Commune of African Descendants, to abide by the decisions of the JFC. Eight representatives, one from each of the eight families, made up the JFC. Their even number meant there were no tie breakers; the members talked, argued and studied until there was unanimous agreement based on the laws of the Commune AND righting injustices of the past.

For example, if an awakened sleeper could not acclimate into the Commune, the awakened son would be released to the outside. This option for those who could not acclimate was based on the effect of the injustice experienced by the sleepers in their past lives, and the fact that many could not overcome those effects, even far into the future. Those released to Outside were given financial resources for 60 days, and the use of their names from before. They were quietly released at sunup by the Justice Forward Circle. While the relative was walked to the Barrier, his relatives erased all evidence of his time in the Commune. There were no ceremonies and no presence from the sleeper's family.

The books had been balanced: the fortune created for families through the sleeping relatives was considered paid in full when relatives were either released to Outside or taken into the Commune. Members of the JFC accompanied the sleeper to the barrier between the Commune and Outside, blessed him and released him with the knowledge that he could never return.

Hester got up and nodded to the new brother. "Are you meeting your relatives for the afternoon walk?" she asked.

Jason shook his head. "I am sensing," he said carefully using the language of the Commune, "that Althea and Nicholas need time without me. I will keep working," he added.

Hester smiled sternly. "Afternoon walks are necessary for balance, mental refreshing and connection. Would you like to join my mother and me?"

Jason admired Hester's work, and honesty wanted to know more about her. *There were so many rules here,* he thought. He looked at her questioningly, wondering if it was alright.

Hester knew. "It will be fine. You should meet some people outside of your family, and my mother loves meeting those new to the Commune."

As he left the lab with Hester, he was once again struck by the beauty of the Commune. There were walking trails and peaceful streams of water everywhere. The sounds, sights and feel of the sun was like nothing he could remember.

As they started on the trail, he noticed Hester's face light up as a dignified woman walked towards them.

"Mother, this is the new son of Althea." Facing Jason, Hester said, "My Brother, please meet my mother, Laura."

Jason took Laura's extended hand. "It's nice to meet you, and kind to allow me to join you on your walk," he said.

Laura turned a piercing glance toward Jason and held the glance for what seemed like hours. "Finally," she replied, "I am happy to meet you New Son. Let's walk together." Laura slipped between Jason and Hester and the three began to walk the trail.

Jason was lulled into such a peaceful state along the walk that the sound of Laura and Hester's conversation moved to the background. On these walks he wanted to take in everything: the smells, the sounds, the feel of the sun on his face, and the beauty of creation. He was so involved in nature that he didn't hear Laura speaking to him.

"Excuse me, New Son. Did you hear me?"

"I'm sorry," Jason replied. "I don't know how to describe what I feel when I walk around the commune."

Laura looked at him piercingly and said, "Try. Tell me what you see as you walk."

Jason looked around the path and suddenly all the people disappeared, and he was left with, pausing he thought, nature. This nature was like nothing he ever recalled experiencing. It was majestic – unreachable in its expanse, yet oddly near. The sounds that the birds and insects created soothed his emotions. He was aware of the beat of his heart and could feel its rate slowing. Jason stopped to remove his shoes as he had seen others do. Laura and Hester silently joined him.

As they continued walking, Jason said, "Before, my Grandma Ruby talked about heaven; this place where there was no suffering or pain, and that was beautiful beyond man's comprehension. The closest way to describe what I am seeing and feeling is how she described heaven. My grandmother lived her life so that one day, after she died, she would get to see a place like this." A single tear escaped Jason's eye, and he didn't attempt to stop its downward path to his chin.

They continued walking in silence, connected by the sense that an important exchange was happening that could not be measured in words. After some time, Jason heard the singing and laughter of children. The trio was approaching the Commune of Elders and Children. Much of the childlike laughter, he realized, came from the elders who attended to the learning of the children. He stopped to observe the interaction and to try to grasp what was happening to him. He saw an elderly man explaining the principles of geometry to children who appeared to be seven or eight years old. The children enthusiastically asked to solve the problem which had been presented by Babu. Jason wondered to himself, *How did children of seven or eight years old understand geometry?* As if reading his thoughts, Laura said, "The elders get to work with the children from their area of expertise. That Babu is one of the engineers of the gardens within the commune. We admire their aesthetics, but if you could see beneath the ground, you would understand the extreme precision necessary to allow earth to be earth without the previously toxic interference of humans.

Jason had a sudden, intense longing to sit with the elders and children. He wanted to be comforted and nourished by those who seemed so much like his grandmother that he imagined he could hear her voice in one of the singing Bibis. He was pierced by the memory of Allan from The Farm as he watched Babu teaching, and overcome with another, more powerful wave of emotion. *What is happening to me?* he thought.

Laura steered Jason to a nearby bench. She whispered something to Hester who disappeared. Laura sat next to Jason, quietly at first. "Hester will be back shortly with Dandelion tea. Perhaps I can help you understand what is happening right now." Laura continued, "You are currently a man of two worlds. The world of Before had its own sights, sounds, communities. Before was very different from here, and some who have come from there cannot acclimate here. What you are experiencing is a war for your spirit. Even though you are generations removed from Before, your experiences still have a stain on your heart. If you are to survive here, you must remove the stains of Before."

"Why were you so moved at the Commune of Elders and Children," Laura continued.

Jason slowly removed an envelope from his inside pocket. He always kept Ruby's letter with him as a reminder that it was she who had made provisions for him to be here, now. He looked at Laura, wondering if he could trust her with the letter he had shared with no one else. He paused, and then handed the letter to her, nodding that she should read it.

After reading the letter, Laura returned it to Jason. "Your grandmother was brave and resourceful. The lives from Before have followed others here. The sorrow and anguish of that time has left such a stain that they cannot comprehend a new life, a new time, a new world. Those unwilling to learn new ways of being cannot survive the Commune of African Descendants. The peace here unnerves them. The joy in children makes them angry for the childhood they didn't have. They are unwilling to accept the gift their relative sacrificed to give them. We do not hold those here who cannot live within the grace and peace we have built. Like the meticulously engineered gardens that were designed to allow God's nature to be showcased in full glory, so our society's order has also been meticulously designed to honor our roles in creation and purpose. We are a purposed people, full of the beauty and creativity of God. We respect the uniqueness that God designed each person with, and we make room for that uniqueness here. To experience the peace and beauty of the Commune, you must choose in which world you will live."

Hester returned to see her mother in deep conversation with Jason. Her mother had such a sense about people, but rarely did she speak to those who had not been embraced fully into the Commune. She told Hester it was too heartbreaking to see them leave if they could not acclimate.

"I brought you some tea," Hester said.

Jason looked at her gratefully as he nodded and accepted the gift.

"I will continue my walk now" Laura said rising. "I will see you at dinner, Daughter." Looking at Jason, "You may call me Aunty," she said as she quickly turned and walked away.

Hester sat down. "Drink your tea while it is cool."

Jason nodded and took a sip. "Even the dandelions taste heavenly here."

They both laughed.

Hester said tentatively, "My mother doesn't take to new people well. In fact, she's rather standoffish. You two must have had quite a conversation."

Jason turned to face Hester. "This place has an effect on me. The beauty of walking the grounds, before today, was just a beautiful walk. As we passed by the Commune of Elders and Children though, I was overcome with longing for the people I've lost- my Grandma Ruby and a man named Allan that I met on The Farm that kept me safe. He taught me things, like planting and work I had not done before. In his rough way, he showed me kindness – the kind you get from a man who cares about your future. I never got to say goodbye to either of them. Seeing the joy on the children's faces and the faces of the older people, I realized I had never experienced that joy or seen it on the faces of those I knew. I wish Grandma Ruby could see this place. I wish I could have let Allan know that I'm alright."

Hester thought to offer some consoling words, but Jason stood abruptly.

"We should get back to the lab. Are you coming?"

Disappointed, Hester got up and the two walked in silence back from the afternoon walk.

The concerns of her heart and the messages in her dreams were validated by Nicholas' words and tone on the walk today. Something was very amiss. Nicholas' tone was patronizing and dismissive. When Althea asked about his sleep and work, he said "Everything is fine. I am learning much from Elder Benjamin." He was obviously spending more time with Benjamin, and Althea wasn't sure how she felt about that.

Benjamin had attempted a romantic relationship with her an acceptable time after her husband's passing, but there was no chemistry. Althea wasn't interested in a romantic relationship, especially when she was still getting over the heartbreak of losing her husband and focused on raising her young son to lead the family one day.

"Well, share with me what you are learning from Elder Benjamin. He is always looking for ways to bring wealth into the Commune. Are there new inventions or discoveries on the horizon?" Althea asked, hoping to spark Nicholas' excitement.

"Nothing that I am at liberty to share right now, Mother. But I will soon," Nicholas responded.

Oh yes, Nicholas thought, *everyone will know what I'm working on very soon.*

Nicholas had always been withdrawn. He didn't seek out friendships with others as a child, or as a youth. His focus had always been on becoming an adult as soon as possible. He excelled in his studies of business and history.

He understood both concepts well, and Althea hoped a career as an instructor or justice official would give him an appreciation for the history and necessity of maintaining the Commune of African Descendants. Nicholas preferred the company of books to people. Althea hoped he would grow out of it, but instead he became even more inwardly focused. Other than Benjamin and his sons, Nicholas had no other friends or associates. He wasn't thinking of marriage either. He always said, "Mother, I will marry once I am successful in my own eyes."

Althea was concerned that without a balanced mindset, Nicholas would never see his own success no matter how much he achieved. Althea felt the weight of the barrier between her and her son. This was different though; more sinister. A mother knows. Something was wrong.

Nicholas and Elder Benjamin had developed a strategy that would remove both Althea and the New Son from any position of influence within the Commune of African Descendants. Once the plan came to fruition, Jason could take his old name back as he was escorted to the outside of the Commune, and Althea would be proven to have diminished capacity for her poor judgment in awakening him. She could go to the Commune of Transition and keep Elder Benjamin's brother company until they both finished their life process.

The only challenge to their plan was figuring out how to get Jason – Nicholas called him by name when speaking with Benjamin and in his own thoughts – to a meeting with the outside. So far Jason had only shown interest in the lab and farm. Under the guise of being mentored, Benjamin would introduce Jason to his contacts outside to give him a better understanding of The Commune's business ventures. Benjamin would talk to Richard and get his help with this sting. Farmington Corporation existed to make money and take care of the unfortunately destitute. For extra money into Farmington's coffers, Benjamin was sure he could convince Richard to be part of their plan.

At first Nicholas didn't think the plan would work. Richard seemed to be an untested variable to him, but Benjamin seemed pretty confident, perhaps because he had known Richard longer.

He and Farmington had been in business together for five years. Still, to Nicholas, Richard seemed to just put up with them for the money; he wasn't sure the man would do anything extra to help them.

Nicholas would give the plan more thought after the meeting today with Benjamin and Richard. Benjamin was leaving it up to Nicholas to start the demise of his mother and new brother.

chapter 39: richard

The seeds from The Farm were all awakened by the same man within months of each other. The seeds were not awakened by family members, but by a board member of FFI who had been bought and paid for. In order for Family Futures Incorporated to be profitable, as many families as possible needed to invest in their cryotechnology. Because of the richness of land in The Farm network, members were able to purchase a shadow board member, someone without voting rights, but with influence. This shadow seat had one job: to show up 160 years after being frozen and wake up The Farm's "seeds". No one at FFI knew the identity of the board member, but they were bound to obey any and all of his requests.

The Farmington Corporation's board of directors was made up of these "Seeds." Their responsibility was to carry the mission of The Farm forward into the future. Those old farmers were smart. They bet on the fact that discrimination, crime and racism would be even more rampant in the future. Richard smiled ironically, they won that bet. The Seeds represented each of The Farm's eight locations and area of expertise. Richard was Chairman of the Board and responsible for keeping Farmington profitable. On weekends, he visited one of the training centers and did some old-fashioned, backbreaking manual labor.

The Seeds of Farmington had one big thing in common; they were all from another time. They had several smaller things in common: none had family, their criminal backgrounds still served them, and they were well set financially by The Farm.All they had to do was their job- saving the people of today who represented their own pasts.

Earlier in the board meeting, Richard had expressed his discomfort with the representatives from the Commune of African Descendants. He wondered aloud if they should put a representative between Farmington and the Commune members. While they all agreed the products from the Commune were invaluable to Farmington's clients, they left how to deal with the shadow man and his team up to Richard.An additional representative from the outside would have to be paid, which would cut into their profits, and none of them wanted that.

Myron, who was responsible for strategy and subterfuge, asked if we needed to assign someone to follow and watch Bennie. The problem was that no one from Outside could breach the barrier of the Commune of African Descendants. None of them had ever been inside the Commune. The only other people they had access to from the commune were the new guy, Nick, or one of Bennie's sons. Jim Bob (this nickname started as a joke, until it stuck), and Derrell talked about assigning someone to watch Bennie's sons. The sons knew none of them but could probably identify Richard. That was a thought. Bennie's sons were responsible for other shadow business dealings Outside.

Jim Bob had been feeling antsy for some action, so the group agreed to let him follow Bennie's sons to see what they could learn about the shadow man's influence.

Somewhat more comfortable, Richard agreed to a meeting with Bennie, Nick and some *New Son.*

chapter 40: nicholas

Nicholas noticed that Jason didn't seem to believe his change of heart. The man's body posture was tense and unreceptive. Perhaps, Nick thought, this was just some holdover behavior from his past – another reason sleepers shouldn't be here. They just didn't fit.

"As I was saying, My Brother, we got off to a bad start. I apologize and would like the chance to be the brother you need. Where should we start?"

Jason thought, *Just because you all woke me up a few months ago doesn't mean I'm stupid.*

This guy was setting off ALL of Jason's alarms. Apparently the instincts that had kept him safe from Before still worked here.Jason didn't want to tip his hand by handing Nick his...backside. That wasn't done here, he supposed. He would play along with Nick until he figured out what was happening.

"Well, tell me about what you do here in The Commune," Jason started.

Nick smiled and thought, *Gotcha!*

"I would be happy to talk about my work and learn more about what you're doing. Shall we start with a walk?"

The two started walking along the path that had become familiar to Jason. He loved the peace of the afternoon walk.

Nicholas began, "You realize that the richness of the Commune doesn't just come from plants and medicine, right?"

"I wasn't sure where the wealth came from here," Jason replied.

"Everything seems to be self-contained, an economy all its own. Am I correct? he continued.

"Yes and no," Nick responded.

"If you're open to it, I will take you on a sort of field trip outside The Commune. Just like any other society, we have formed relationships with other communities that are mutually beneficial. Would you like to see what the outside looks like?"

Nick watched Jason carefully, hoping to determine whether his instincts were right about the sleeper.

Jason seemed to ponder the invitation and then asked, "Isn't there a rule against Awakened Citizens going outside before their naming ceremony?"

Nick had already considered that question. He replied in a confidential tone, "Under normal circumstances that's true. But we are the sons of the Family Elder, so we need to determine where your talents can best serve The Commune. We have greater freedom to explore opportunities than most others. If it will make you comfortable, I will clear it with mother."

Jason replied, "If Althea approves, I would love to learn more about what you do and to see the outside. Thank you for inviting me."

Both men continued walking, each with his own thoughts. Nick had crossed the first hurdle in his plan to eliminate Jason as Althea's possible successor and member of their family. If his instincts were correct, breaking the rule about leaving The Commune would discredit Jason with the Commune.

Exposing him as the front man for their illicit dealings would destroy his reputation with both Althea and those who were watching his progress. He would revisit the plan with Benjamin by first making sure his contacts would deal with Jason. After that, he would learn more about Jason's past life to find what he could use to trap him into going back to that life in this time.

Jason didn't believe for one minute that Nick wanted to suddenly *be a brother* to him. He knew that Nick was jealous of him for reasons he didn't understand. He also didn't believe it was acceptable for him to go outside The Commune, but if Nick spoke to Althea and she allowed it, Jason wanted to see what the world outside looked like. The Commune was beautiful, peaceful and almost heavenly. In spite of the family connections, Jason still didn't feel he belonged. *What might it be like to live outside?* Jason was curious enough to ignore the warnings he felt to find out.

When the two of them came to the lab where Jason had been working, Nick said,

"I'll talk with mother and let you know at dinner about the trip outside. Just in case, I will also speak with Elder Benjamin to assure Althea that everything will be fine."

Jason nodded and went into the lab to start work.

chapter 41: althea

Althea watched from the quiet space of her dwelling as her two sons started an afternoon walk together. She had prayed for this, but instead of being happy, she felt a sense of foreboding, like she was watching the unfolding of Cain and Abel. Althea shuddered as she remembered her dream. To think that the child she bore and nurtured all his life would become her betrayer was too much to bear. *Would it be easier for her heart if the betrayal came from her new son?* She turned and looked toward the Commune of Elders and Children. How her heart longed for the peace and joy of teaching the coming generations. Her fear that she would not join them soon was her second most pressing fear.

Althea's biggest fear was that she would die alone and rejected by her son, without heirs to continue their family line. She feared that her son would discredit and reject her so that he could become Family Elder. A son who would do such a thing would not be fit to serve on the Council of Families. The Council would be tainted going forward by her own flesh and blood. The impact of Nick on the Council would change how Families and The Commune met the future. Althea knew that Nick had become attached to Elder Benjamin's family and was pivotal in trade with the outside. She wasn't sure that Nick, given his character flaws, could maintain a stance of integrity when dealing with those who adhered to the standards outside.

Althea was putting much of her heart and hope in Jason. She prayed that the instructions to wake him were from above and not her fears within.She watched him in the laboratory and saw his quick mind and curiosity. The new son was learning their ways, and she imagined it was a complicated learning process. To be sent four generations into the future, to a world so vastly different from what one has known, was beyond her imagination.

Yet, he was adapting. He had even gained some grudging respect from Laura of the Justice Forward Circle – that was no small feat. Althea had been friends with Laura for many years and knew the woman to be an insightful and observant judge of character.

Althea and Laura had seen each other through the most difficult times of each of their lives. When Althea's husband died, Laura was the friend who walked with her through the days of tears and questioning. When Althea refused to eat, it was Laura who not only brought food, but motivation as to why Althea must live. Sadly, Althea had done the same thing for Laura. During the fight to keep her husband, Raphael, as family elder on the Council of Families, coming to grips with his declining mental health was almost as bad as death. The strain of watching the man you love castigated by his family and friends would have sent Laura into a dark depression if not for her friend, Althea. The two women had a long and deep history.

When Laura said, "I am excited about our new son's presence here. I believe he will help lead us into the future," Althea breathed a grateful sigh. Laura didn't make those kinds of pronouncements unless she had run a person's character through her extensive filters. As Althea remembered Laura's words, her spirit lifted. She had not made a mistake in waking the new son. She just hoped Nicholas would open his heart to the possibilities of them being a real, loving family.

chapter 42: jason

Jason was conflicted. He enjoyed the peace and work in The Commune, but he was driven to learn about the Outside. He wondered if this was the problem the awakened had that caused them to get put out of The Commune. The idea that Nicholas and others had work out there was intriguing; might there be work for him in and outside of The Commune as well? Nicholas still set off alarms inside of him. No matter what he said, Jason knew there was an ulterior motive at work. He would play along with Nicholas' plan.

Jason approached Althea without telling her about Nicholas' invitation. When he asked her how he should decide where his work would be she told him, "Follow where your heart, intellect and curiosity lead you." Well, today was the day that his heart, intellect and curiosity would find out about Outside.

Jason met Nicholas, Elder Benjamin and his two sons at the designated walkway near the wall separating The Commune from Outside.

"I forgot to tell you," Nicholas started, "for your own protection we need you to wear a hood. You are still new and what we are doing will keep you and The Commune safe."

Jason didn't like it.

Elder Benjamin, sensing his hesitance replied, "Just until we get you inside the transport vehicle; then we'll remove the hood. We can't let anything happen to you or Althea would never forgive us.

This is for your protection so that no one recognizes you." Benjamin then whispered conspiratorially, "And you know that it is against Commune rules for you to be outside the wall before your naming day. We are protecting you from being seen."

Jason acquiesced. He put his hand on Nicholas' arm and was led out of the Commune wearing the hood.

As the car – that's what Jason assumed it was – started to move, Nicholas removed the hood. Looking through the tinted windows Jason noticed the gradual and then drastic change in appearance from the grounds of The Commune to Outside. This was familiar to Jason. Almost instantly the sounds and sights of the past came rushing back into his consciousness – hitting his head and gut like a hammer. The effect was briefly dizzying. Shaking his head, he regained his composure and looked around. Benjamin and Nicholas were staring at him intently, while Benjamin's sons talked as if nothing was happening.

"Are you ill?", Benjamin asked. "I noticed a change in your energy."

"Not ill," Jason replied. "Just overwhelmed for a moment with what looks very familiar. I'm fine now."

The car pulled to a stop. Benjamin spoke to his sons, "We'll meet back here in two hours. I want to make sure Jason gets a full tour of our business out here. Don't make us wait for you or you'll have to find your own way back to The Commune."

Benjamin's oldest son smirked, "We'll be here."

The two men left the car and disappeared down a side street for their meeting.

Jason was fascinated as the car pulled in front of The Farmington Corporation. This was a corporation, much like those he imagined himself working in his past life. Perhaps these business arrangements were legitimate and right. A nervous excitement started to build in Jason as he realized he was about to learn how The Commune interacted with those outside. For a euphoric moment, Jason believed Nicholas really would be a brother to him.

The euphoria changed to bewilderment as Jason came face to face with the killer he had known in his old life as Rico.

chapter 43: collision

The group was greeted by a woman who led them into a well-appointed conference room, where at the head of the table stood the man who had been his closest friend 200 years in the past. Benjamin took it upon himself to make the introductions:

"Jason, well that's his name from the past. He hasn't had his naming ceremony yet, so this meeting has to be discreet. Jason, this is Richard. Richard is chairman of the board of The Farmington Corporation. The Farmington Corporation is one of our most valued business partners on the Outside. Richard, this is Jason. He is a new son in The Commune, and brother to Nicholas."

There it was, Jason thought. The subtle shake of Richard's head which told him to play along. Yes, this was his childhood friend, and their cues still worked.

"I hope we can continue a profitable business relationship with you, Jason", Richard said.

"I look forward to learning from Nicholas, Benjamin and you," Jason replied.

The men shook hands and the subtle twist at the end of the handshake wasn't noticed by the others in the room.

Jason and Rico were together again.

chapter 44: laura

Laura was preparing for her regular visit to Raphael in the Community of Transition. She shrugged off the sympathetic glances of friends and neighbors who only meant well. Laura knew the truth, and playing along with the charade was getting more difficult. As she was preparing to leave, Hester stopped her.

"Mother, can we have a conversation about the New Son?"

Laura stopped and patted the cushion next to her. Examining her daughter, she asked, "What is your concern?"

Hester seemed uncharacteristically nervous.

"Mother, I believe Uncle Benjamin and Nicholas are going to sabotage the New Son.

Laura put her thoughts of Raphael away and focused. "What do you mean sabotage?", she asked.

Hester struggled with betraying the uncle who loved her with what she was about to say. "I overheard Uncle Benjamin talking with Marcus and Edwin about his plans to move Althea as family elder by setting up the New Son with an Outside group. They didn't know I was in the house. Mother, it sounds like they are about to entrap the New Son into something he knows nothing about. I don't want to be fearful, but hearing the conversation made me afraid for what might happen in The Commune." Hester breathed.

It seemed to Laura that Hester had been holding her breath for a very long time.

"When did you overhear this conversation? Can you tell me the details of what you heard?", Laura asked.

When Hester finished talking almost an hour later, Laura knew exactly who to share this information with.

Stringing beads. Raphael felt all his days amounted to beads strung and naps. Playing the role of a demented elder was hard, but doing otherwise would put his family in danger. Raphael knew that his brother would make good on his promise to give the poison pills to Laura and Hester if anyone discovered his plans. Raphael had been in the Commune of Transition for more than a year. The staff remarked about his vitality and mental acuity -- for a demented man. The theater training of his youth served him well in his current role.

He noticed the time. Laura was late. It wasn't like her to be late for their visits; she knew how much they meant to him. Something must be wrong. Just as Raphael was about to demand more time in the recreation room, he saw Laura's frame walking up the path.

Great, he thought. *Time to get tired and be taken to my room.*

Speaking to the nurse, he said loudly, "Too noisy. Too noisy here. I want to leave!" he said in a raised, booming voice. She smiled softly, touched Raphael's shoulder, and directed one of the aids to wheel him to his quarters.

Once in his quarters, Raphael could drop the façade. He breathed an exhausted sigh and stood as Laura slipped into the door. She ran to him, as she always did, and kissed him softly.

"I miss you every day," she said.

Raphael smiled. He lived for his time with Laura; it was the only time he didn't have to pretend to be unwell.

"How are you, my love?", he asked.

Laura looked at him sternly and said, "We're going to have to move our plans up."

chapter 46: rico

Rico ushered Bennie and his team out to the waiting car. He watched from the window as they put the hood over Jason's head and led him into the backseat. Rico was conflicted, *How in the hell did Jason wind up in this time with him? Who was Bennie to Jason, and what was that crook up to*? Most importantly, Rico wondered if the rules of engagement concerning his old friend still mattered, or if he was to treat Jason like any other stranger.

Nobody could have seen this coming. Rico tried to imagine what Will and the men from The Farm would want. After all, when they couldn't get Jason back, they had kidnapped Rico in his place. Jason knew the rules of The Farm and its purpose. Could Rico trust Jason with the secret to The Farmington Corporation? Was Jason still the same person after all this time?

Rico knew he wouldn't sleep tonight. He let the woman at the front know that he was going to the woodshop colony to work off some frustration.

chapter 47: jason

Jason nodded and asked questions on the ride back to make Benny and Nicholas think he was interested. Really, though, his mind was spinning. How did Rico get here? How is it that he was face to face with a man who should have died at least 200 years ago? He didn't understand how this time worked. There were people sent here from the past who weren't part of The Commune? It felt like too much.

When the car stopped in front of his and Nicholas' quarters, Jason could barely control his emotions.

He looked Nicholas in the eye and said, "Thank you for teaching me what you do. I want to learn more, and I hope that is ok."

Nicholas smiled. "Of course, my brother. I will teach you what you need to know so that you can succeed."

And to Jason's surprise, Nicholas hugged him. Now the alarm bells were going non-stop. The two men parted ways to their individual quarters: Jason to think, and Nicholas to advance his plan.

Althea watched as her sons returned together.She caught her breath as she saw Nicholas initiate a hug. She watched them and for the first time since he had been awakened, she hoped for a future that included both sons as leading members of their family. She pushed back the troubling thought of what sparked the change in Nicholas' behavior.

hester

Hester was starting to look forward to the daily walks with the new son. She enjoyed discovering his intellect and hearing what he valued most in The Commune. When she spoke of her own passions, he listened with an intensity of one who is discovering a new world, but who also possesses wisdom from another time. Hester could picture Jason building blocks from his past that connected to his present so that he could find his place within both.

Jason noticed what looked like nervousness in Hester. He had never observed that in their interactions.

He asked, tentatively, "Is something concerning you?"

Jason used careful, distinct words. He normally would have asked, "Is something bothering you?", but nobody knew the word 'bother' here.

"Hester," he gently touched her arm to get her attention.

"Yes," she replied firmly. "Something is concerning me."

She stopped walking and turned to look at Jason.

"I am concerned that Nicholas is not being honest with you about his work, and that he may be attempting to set you up."

Hester started to speak fast, before she lost her nerve to tell all she had heard.

"I overheard a conversation between my Uncle Benjamin and his sons, Marcus and Edwin.

Benjamin was telling them about his plans to move Althea aside as family elder by setting you up in a trap with one of the Outside groups. They didn't know I was in the house. I know you don't know about that part of the business, and that Nicholas has been angry ever since you were awakened. Their conversation sounded bigger than just your family, and it made me afraid for what might happen in The Commune."

Hester took a long breath and looked at Jason directly. She noticed a flicker in his eyes.

"What was that look?" she asked Jason.

Jason wasn't as good as he thought at covering his emotions. He wondered how much he should tell her about his past, and if it would change the way she viewed him. Apparently, it didn't matter. Rico was here and Jason had already been introduced to the "Outside." Whatever Benjamin and Nicholas were conspiring had already begun. Jason took a long breath and steered Hester to a nearby bench.

Sitting next to her he said, "I need to tell you about me."

Two hours later Hester knew Jason's past and how it could be used to entrap him in this present. Jason didn't realize the extent of emotion he would experience sharing everything. Nobody knew everything. Not his grandmother. Not Althea. He corrected the thought: Rico knew everything. If anyone could undo his grandmother's plans for a successful future, it was his friend from the past.

Hester was quiet for what seemed like hours.

Finally, she tentatively asked, "Do you trust me?"

Jason looked at her, uncertain how to answer.

"You know the life I lived. I was just beginning to feel safe, like I might learn a different life. I just learned that the same systems I fought to navigate more than 100 years ago are still in place with upgrades. People are still the same. How do I know who to trust? What happens to me if I trust the wrong people. Will I be tossed "Outside" with my old name, some money and a 200 year old 'gotcha'? As you can see, from where I sit, the issue of trust is a life or death question for me. I need some time myself. I'm sorry. I just don't know."

Jason stood and responded in a politely cordial tone, "I am returning to my quarters now for some meditation time."

He had heard others use that phrase when they needed time alone.

Hester stood and nodded, mirroring Jason's politeness.

"It was a pleasure getting to know you. Rest well."

As she walked away, Hester knew exactly where she was going and to whom she would speak.

Laura listened intently to Hester. She noticed the tremors in her daughter's voice, observed how she fidgeted with the edge of her sleeve. Hester was emotionally involved with the new son, otherwise she would not be so affected. As Laura listened, she understood Hester's emotions weren't the primary concern.There were two concerns much more pressing. First, what Benjamin was attempting could alter the way the Commune of African Descendants operated.

To have an elder overseeing two families and who was engaged in illegal activities would undermine the core values of The Commune.The second problem is that Laura would have to come clean with Hester about her father's real condition. They were going to need his help.

Raphael took a deep breath after Laura shared their daughter's concerns. He knew his brother. Benjamin was not trying to help Nicholas become Family Elder; he was setting himself up to oversee two families. Raphael had been victim to Benjamin's lies when the man took oversight of their own family. He knew what the man was capable of, and of his ruthless greed. Raphael had always suspected Benjamin of making additional profits above what he stated on the outside business contracts. He had taught his sons to do business the same way, secretly and unethically. When Raphael, as older brother, had confronted Benjamin about his suspicions and threatened to expose him, the smear campaign started.

Raphael had the rare combination of business acumen and creative eccentrics. He was able to relate to both those governed by the left and right sides of the brain. Benjamin's campaign to discredit Raphael started with exaggerating his creative inclinations with phrases like, "He spends too much time dialoging with himself about the arts," or "He's starting to stare off into space a lot." Benjamin convinced one of the physicians that Raphael was in steep mental decline. The convincing took some financial incentive, but the doctor eventually examined his brother and recommended he be transferred into the Commune of Transition.

Raphael could either agree to go to the Commune, or risk having his family humiliated or harmed, and at the very least, Laura losing her position due to the public, nasty battle that would ensue between the brothers.

Raphael considered Laura his greatest gift and asset.When the battle between the brothers came to a head, Raphael and Laura spent six months acclimating themselves to the new reality of their lives. They both had to play a role if Raphael was ever to be released. They couldn't even let their daughter know that Raphael was not in decline. That night they agreed to tell Hester about her father's true condition. Laura felt lighter than she had in two years. This nightmare without her husband and family intact was about to come to an end. What Hester told her might be a key to bringing Benjamin down, but they needed more than suspicion – they needed to know what Benjamin was doing.

jason

Jason's mind continued to reel as he lay on the sofa in his quarters. Since coming here, he had experienced a sense of both clarity and stability in watching the sunrise. Watching the sunrise reminded him that this was the same sun he and his grandmother had lived under generations ago. In an odd way the sun seemed a bridge between then and now. Lost in his thoughts, he was startled by the gentle tapping on his door. That light tap could only be Althea; she was always very careful about interrupting.

Rising, he opened the door and embraced her. He had never noticed how frail she was physically. Today he felt the bones in her shoulders. Althea had a commanding presence and a strong voice, but in this moment Jason was reminded that she was at least as old as his grandmother had been when she died. They sat together on the couch, and Althea started. "How are you, my son?"

"I am learning much," Jason replied. "There is much more to this time, and the Commune that I became aware of. Today, I am overwhelmed with what I am discovering."

Althea's expression changed to one of concern. "Perhaps I can help. Would you like to ask me questions or share what you are discovering?"

Jason looked deeply into Althea's eyes and realized telling her what Nicholas was planning would break her.

"I want to sort through some things myself. And then I promise, I will let you know everything. You have been so kind to me, kinder than anyone other than my grandmother. I want to ask that you trust me. Whatever I do, know that I am doing it to protect you, ok?"

Althea nodded as she shuddered inwardly. The feeling of dread was back. She realized she could no longer look away from what might be happening within her family. Standing, she touched Jason's cheek. "I understand. I'm going to spend some time in meditation with The Wind for the next few days, so I won't be available. If you need me, though, send a message."

Then like a lightbulb, the idea hit Jason. If Nicholas was trying to set him up, he would use Rico to do it. If Jason could arrange a nudge to get closer to Rico alone, that might seem to give Nicholas the ammunition he needed, while allowing Jason to talk with Rico in private. In order for the plan to work, Jason would need to show more interest in life Outside than his work in the Commune.This would mean showing disinterest in the work he was doing in The Commune.

Realizing he wouldn't be in proximity to Hester bothered him in a way he didn't expect. They had a shared interest in their work, and that shared interest seemed to be turning into something else. Hester had asked if he trusted her. Now it was time to find out.

Walking through the park to the Laboratory where they had spent much of their time, Jason was nervous. He realized finding out he couldn't trust Hester would cut deeper than he had experienced. In his old life, his circle had been small and tight – there was no room for romantic associations. While he wasn't proud of it, Jason recognized all his interactions with female partners had been transactional. They lacked the emotional and spiritual connection necessary for a committed relationship. The connection he had with Hester felt emotional and spiritual, and that made him very nervous.

Lost in thought, Jason nearly collided with Hester on the way into the laboratory. Hester was returning from what appeared to be a solitary walk.

"Oh, sorry," Jason said. "I was coming to talk about your question. Do you have a few minutes to sit?"

Hester nodded silently and moved toward one of the benches just outside the lab. After nervously fidgeting with her sleeve, Hester took a deep breath and looked directly at Jason, still not speaking.

Jason started, "I never had to examine whether I trusted someone or not. In my old life I kept my circle small and tight. There were my two best friends, Rico and Monster, and my grandmother. That was my circle. My world was made-up of the work that I did in the streets and taking care of my grandmother. That was my whole world until one day I was kidnapped and taken to The Farm, which changed my life and led me here. Will you be patient enough to let me tell you part of what I believe is happening, and then to trust that what I do to find out more is in the best interest of the commune?"

Hester nodded.

Jason continued. "You heard me mention my friend Rico. Brace yourself for what comes next. The other day when I went out with Benjamin and Nicholas, the person that you're doing business with on the outside is my old friend Rico. How he is here is a mystery to me. When I went into the conference room of Farmington Corporation, I didn't know what to expect, but seeing Rico threw me. I told you about my past. Rico was the coldest killer you would ever meet, but he was also my childhood friend. We met in Sunday School. I know his history. He was the closest thing to a brother I had back then, and he recognizes me the same now.

Knowing that he is leading an organization I suspect is doing shady business with Nicholas and Benjamin makes me think the Commune could be in danger. Can I trust you to keep this quiet while I pursue some time with Rico to find out what's going on?"

Hester examined Jason for what seemed like hours. Then she said quietly, "You can trust me, if I can trust you. Don't do anything until after tomorrow and keep this conversation and what follows quiet."

"It's time for you to meet my father."

Laura and Althea had known each other a long time and shared both joys and pain, so when she needed a sounding board for what she was sensing, Althea sought out her friend. Walking together in the early evening, Althea noticed Laura seemed both emotionally light and mentally heavy at the same time. Both women observed strict levels of respect for the other's work, so they never pried from that perspective.

Althea spoke first. "I know we are here because I need to discuss some concerns I am having, but is there something weighing on your mind?"

Laura looked at her old friend, touching her shoulder.

"Yes, there are some things on my mind, but you go first."

Althea took a deep breath and started to speak. As she spoke, tears came from her eyes, though the tone and authority of her voice were unchanged.

"I am questioning If I made the right decision in waking Jason. You know that my desire was to transition into the community of elders and children, but Nicholas is not ready to be our families elder, and I'm not sure he ever will. I hoped that he and Jason could work together to build a strong family, establish their own families, and ensure that our line would continue. Nicholas has only expressed interest in leadership, not the family.

And while I know he is your brother-in-law, I am concerned about his relationship with Benjamin. There are some things happening with his business dealings that while I am not aware of, I don't trust.”

Althea looked at her friend, and noticing no offense, she continued.

“I hoped that Jason and Nicholas would become brothers in spirit. In fact, I have spent some time alone in prayer, and something is not right. After my time with The Wind and in meditation, I come to you -- most trusted friend --with the concerns of my heart. If my son Nicholas is involved in business outside that would harm the commune, what might his consequences be, in a worst-case scenario?”

Laura nodded. She could hear the worry in her friend's voice and see it in her disposition.

“The consequences would depend on the motive, and the level of premeditation involved in the arrangements. I'm sure we would take into consideration any other influences your son might have encountered. Let me ask you Althea, what do you believe is happening? We've known each other for a long time, and I've never known you to be given to wild imaginations. What is your spirit telling you?”

Althea responded quickly, “I believe Nicholas is engaging in some activity to gain power and become the lead elder by dishonest means. I also believe that somehow Benjamin will benefit if that happens...”

Althea's expression changed, “I am standing in the way of what Nicholas wants. How far do you think he would go to become elder? Do you think my own son might be willing to harm me?”

Laura's disposition swiftly changed to that of a member of the powerful Justice Forward Circle. Her tone was low and intense, "You have warned me of potential criminal activity. If you feel safe, we can watch and prepare to move. Right now, we have no proof of criminal activity, but we can begin an investigation. Just based on what you're saying though, I think we need to do this quickly to keep you out of any possible danger."

Althea hugged her friend as fresh tears flowed, "Do what you can to protect my sons. Both of them, please."

The two friends sat in silence for a few minutes, both considering the burden they were now living with. They squeezed hands, got up from the bench and walked silently to their own dwellings.

nicholas

Nicholas and Benjamin met at Benjamin's dwelling like they normally did. Nicholas was excited because he saw the plan to become chief elder coming into place. Jason had asked to know more about the business they did with Farmington Corporation. Nicholas had offered to set up a meeting with just Jason and Richard. After a few of these meetings, Nicholas would have the evidence to give to the rest of the family of Jason's betrayal of Commune principles. Because it was Althea who had awakened Jason, the lapse in judgement would make the case for her diminished mental capacity. This would be the first powerful nail in her coffin as Family Elder.

Benjamin was pleased with the progression of their plan.He had negotiated an increase in their sales to Farmington Corporation with the understanding that when he became Family Elder of two families, the price would be reduced. Richard would have a vested interest in helping them so that he could keep a healthy bottom line for Farmington. As for Jason and Nicholas? Who cared. Jason would be sent to live Outside for his betrayal of Commune principles. If Nicholas didn't agree to allow Benjamin to take over his family from Althea, he could go live with Jason. His partnerships on the outside with both Farmington Corp and other illegal activities would allow him to manufacture whatever evidence he needed to get what he wanted.

chapter 50: rico

Rico hadn't slept since he had met Jason the week before. How could this be? He had left the office every day and gone directly to the wood shop or the farm to attempt to work himself to exhaustion. His body was tired, but his mind would not stop racing. Jason was here in this time. They had crossed each other's paths again. Their old handshake from the past established that they still recognized each other. But who was Jason in this time, and was he here to destroy or build the connection between The Commune and Farmington Corporation? As if in answer to his questions, the communication device announced a call from Benjamin.

"Richard," he started without preamble, "I wonder if you can do us a favor. The New Son, uh, I mean Jason, wants to know more about our business with you. Would you mind meeting with him to uh…explain things?"

Rico smiled. "I would be happy to, Benjamin. Anything that will help our business together."

"Great," Benjamin said. "We'll drop him off around noon tomorrow. We have other business in the area to attend to." Rico ended the conversation and thought, *From my lips to God's ears.*

He buzzed the woman at the front desk and asked her to clear his calendar tomorrow afternoon.

raphael

Laura, Hester and Jason sat uncomfortably in the community room of the Commune of Transition.

"Who are you again," Raphael asked impatiently.

Laura interrupted, "Sweetheart, this is a New Son, a friend of Hester's."

Raphael made a sucking sound with his mouth. He then yelled to the attendants, "I want to go to my room. These people are nice friends of my wife. Can they come too? I want a story!"

The nurse smiled and patted Raphael's shoulder.

"Are you sure you aren't too tired for company?"

Raphael took a deep breath and exploded: "I want to go to my room. I want my wife's friends to come because they're going to read me a STORY!"

The nurse looked questioningly at Laura.

"It's ok," she mouthed. "We'll tell him a story, and I will get him tucked in. Thank you so much."

As the four of them headed towards Raphael's room,

Hester commented "That was quite a performarce, Father."

When her mother took her to visit a few days ago and she learned of her father's true condition, she could have floated with happiness. She knew their family had to keep up the pretense for their own safety, but life felt much better. Life also felt much better because she could see a deeper connection growing between her and Jason. She wanted to laugh at his nervousness. He hadn't been told of Raphael's true condition yet.

As they entered his quarters, a seriousness came over Raphael's face. He looked sternly at Jason and said, "My family trusts you. No one in the commune outside of those in this room knows that I'm well. Let me tell you how I got here. My brother, the man you know as Benjamin, built a case of diminished capacity against me so that he could become the chief elder of our family. His word would never have been enough to put me here, but he had influence with a physician and those outside the commune to create the trail of evidence that convinced our family of my current mental illness and impending death.

"As you can see," Raphael chuckled, "Reports of my demise have been highly exaggerated."

At the end of that quote, Raphael laughed with Rachel and Hester.

"Now first things first," he said, reverting to seriousness: "What is your interest in my daughter?"

After a short, but uncomfortable silence, Jason said, "I am drawn to your daughter's care for the Commune and her desire to protect and nourish it. I am captivated by her beauty and compassion. Her intellect fascinates me. She..."

Raphael interrupted, "That's enough."

"So, what of this business with my brother?", Raphael asked.

Jason took a long breath and shared everything he had shared with Hester, including meeting Rico at an "Outside" meeting. Raphael was quiet, studying him.

After a few minutes of silence, Laura spoke. "I believe it is critical to get to the bottom of what is happening because Althea could be in danger. We know how far Benjamin is willing to go to get what he wants," she said pausing and looking at Raphael. "And Nicholas is the perfect tool Benjamin can use to get rid of Althea."

Raphael looked at Jason with a penetrating stare.

"Finally," he spoke. "Whether you intended it or not, Jason we are now family, bound by these secrets. My condition cannot be revealed to anyone until we have unraveled what Benjamin is doing to destroy Althea's influence." Turning to Laura, Raphael asked, "Is there a way Jason can be shielded from the penalty of going Outside if he uncovers criminal behavior by Benjamin or Nicholas?"

Laura nodded.

"Well Son, you cannot come here again until this is over. It would be suspicious for a potential suitor to spend too much time with a young lady's mentally incompetent father. You two are going to have to behave like a courting couple; and you can keep us all advised that way."

"One more thing," Raphael continued, "You represent hope for our family that we haven't had in a long time. If you find evidence of Benjamin's work against the Commune, I can stop pretending and come home. If you can't find anything significant, I will be here until my time runs out. Make whatever you do count, Son.And welcome to The Commune of African Descendants. Please kneel for a blessing."

Jason looked to Hester who had a funny smile on her face, and at Laura who nodded to him through a tearful smile. Jason knelt and Raphael placed his hands on Jason's head. He said a prayer of blessing and welcome, one that was only offered after a New Son had proven himself worthy of the Commune. Jason lifted his head to meet the old man's eyes, and felt the mix of safety, trust and respect that he felt with Allan on the farm, more than 200 years ago. Impulsively, Jason hugged the old man and quickly left Laura and Hester so they wouldn't see his tears.

Nicholas was pleased with how fast Jason was picking up interest in their dealings outside the commune.He had believed it would take a little more coaxing, but his plan was going better than expected. Even Benjamin was impressed with the speed of luring Jason to break Commune rules by getting involved in their *external affairs*. Both Nicholas and Benjamin chuckled at the phrase. Yes, that would be their codename for the operation to both eliminate Althea and elevate Nicholas to the role of chief elder for the family. What Nicholas did not realize was that once Althea was deposed, Benjamin would let everyone know that both Jason and Nicholas were involved externally and would move for both of their dismissal from the Commune. This action would cut off Althea's family line, leaving Benjamin to propose a temporary takeover of the family elder's duties, that would become permanent. He had already accomplished that with his own family leadership. As chief elder of two families within the Commune, Benjamin would become the unquestioned leader of the Commune, even if no one ever referred to him that way.

Benjamin's thoughts were interrupted by the driver who signaled they had arrived at Farmington Corporation. With the plan in place, Nicholas was staying within The Commune and Jason was meeting with Farmington alone. This would remove all doubt that Jason was involved in illegal activities.

Looking to Jason, Benjamin said, "Learn all that you can. The knowledge you gain will help more people in The Commune. Your work here will also help to accelerate you into acceptance here at the Commune." The implication was meant to be unmistakable: this work would propel Jason into favor with those in The Commune. "I will be back at dusk to take you back to the Commune."

jason and rico

The two men stared at each other for what seemed like hours. Jason's mind was reeling from the clash of past memories and the present reality that made this moment possible. Rico was his friend, but was this Richard a friend, foe or something in between?

Jason spoke one word: "How?"

"I could ask you the same thing. First, though, let me start by telling you how I am here as Chairman of Farmington Corporation. That day a long time ago when you came back to the apartment to look for your grandmother, started me on a different journey. A man kidnapped me and took me to a farm in the south. At first, I was scared, because I didn't understand what happened. Gradually, I got used to it and a man named Will started training me to lead. Those old men were a trip!"

Jason interrupted him, "They took you to The Farm? When?"

"Apparently when they lost you," Rico said. You got arrested, and I got taken. Monster got killed that day."

Both men became silent for some time as they remembered Monster's last words: "Greater love."

Rico continued, "I got what the old men were about, and little by little they won me over. I was willing to stay there and build until The Farm system was destroyed. It was bad from what Will said. Each farm was destroyed, the leaders killed, and the land and materials stolen."

Jason stopped and remembered Allan and the other old ones he met on The Farm.

"How did you get away?" he asked softly.

"Those old men had a plan. Each individual farm had *a seed*, a young man who had been identified as a leader. When the call came through that the destroyers were coming, each *seed* was driven off the farm and to FFI. FFI had authorization from a shadow board member to send the seeds forward and establish "The Farm" under a system in line with whatever future world was happening.Those old dudes bet that racism and classism would still be in effect, and they bet right. Each of my board members, leaders of individual areas of Farmington Corporation, is a seed from one of the past farms."

Rico gave Jason a minute to digest it.

"So now, how did you come to be here?"

Jason smiled wryly, "Grandma Ruby," he said. "Apparently my grandmother sold everything she had to get me a ticket to the future. I didn't know as much about my grandmother as I thought I did", he continued.

"In addition to being an early purchaser of the FFI cryotechnology, the farm we both spent time at with Allan and the other men was Grandma Ruby's property."

"Those old people were geniuses," Rico said.

Jason just nodded; his mind was beginning to grasp all the pieces necessary to get Rico and him together, more than 200 years into the future. There was a tension between the two men, though. The nature of their current relationship had yet to be determined. Jason spoke first.

"So, what is your relationship with Benjamin, Nicholas and The Commune? It is obviously not open because the people I know in the Commune don't seem to know about this business. And if your business with the Commune will cause us harm, that puts us on opposite sides."

"To answer your first question, The Commune sells medicines, food and supplies to organizations outside. The difference is those organizations have a similar philosophy of living as the Commune. Our philosophy is different. For example, are you aware that selling narcotics on the street is not illegal today? It is not accepted by everyone, but doctors are only available for the ultra-rich, and medicines are expensive. We sell drugs here, but all of our customers aren't junkies. Some are sick. They can't afford to buy from traditional pharmacies, so they come here to us. The quality of Commune-produced medicines is also out of reach for most people, unless you have someone from inside The Commune willing to make side deals with organizations like Farmington Corporation."

"Our business," Rico continued, "consists of the kind of street operation you and I had back then, and the rehabilitative aspects of The Farm. Before you decide if we're on opposite sides, the Jason I remember would want to know more. Do you want to see our work?"

Rico didn't wait for an answer. Jason followed him out into another conference room where the board of Farmington Corporation waited.

chapter 52: the board meeting

Jason looked at the men seated around the table. They looked like men he would have known in another time.Rico pointed to an empty seat to his left, and Jason sat down. Rico stood at the head of the table.

"It's time for some introductions," he said. "Brothers, I want to introduce you to someone I knew as a friend from Before. I knew him as Jason, and he was in charge of the crew I was part of before The Farm. I confess, I don't know what the nature of our relationship will be going forward, but at Farmington Corporation, we keep the cards on the table with each other." Looking at Jason, Rico continued. "Why don't you introduce yourself and state your business. Once we hear you out, if warranted, I will introduce you to the men around the table; the Board of Farmington Corporation."

Jason cleared his throat and looked at Rico for a few seconds. "I never expected to see someone who had been my best friend in this time. The last things I remember from before was learning my Grandma Ruby had died, and finding my friends", he nodded towards Rico, "Monster and Rico in her apartment when Allan from The Farm brought me to check on her, and then getting arrested and transferred where I got a shot and woke up here. It's a new world here, that's not so different from the one we came from. Yeah, in The Commune the air is clean, the food is healthy, and the people are balanced, mostly. But there's that element, you know.

That underground, beneath the surface place where most of us lived back then. There's a veneer that looks nice and shiny, but I feel like it's covering up something real evil. I think the business Benjamin is involved in with you all has something to do with what's waking up my old instincts."

Jason continued, "I woke up to a family – a matriarch named Althea. She's kind and like an auntie. She has a son, Nicholas, who is not what he seems. He has been an enemy to me until recently. Suddenly he and Benjamin want me to know about their secret business outside. This is suspicious because they don't realize I know it is against Commune rules for me to be out here. I would have respected the rules and kept my nose down, but then I saw Rico and I needed to know more."

Jason felt like he could exhale. "I'll stop now, and you can ask what you want."

Jason turned to Rico, "I'm out here now, and either I will get exiled from the Commune for being here once people find out, or I will find out what Benjamin and Nicholas are up to. Either way, I'm trusting you and hoping you are the same man I stood side by side with before."

Rico broke the silence after a few minutes of thought.

"Well fellas, let's make the introductions and talk about next steps."

He nodded to the man to his left. One by one each man around the table introduced himself and what they did for Farmington Corporation.

"Calvin, Manufacturing."

"Ross - Engineering."

"Derrell - People Management."

A few of the men snickered.

"People management?", Calvin said.

"Interesting description."

"Mind ya' business," Derrell said.

"People Management. Now who's next?"

"Myron – Strategic..uh..research. Yeah, that's it."

There were more snickers around the table but no comments.

"Isaiah – Communications."

"My name is Jim Bob, and I am responsible for Street Team Oversight. Don't ask me about my name."

Laughter broke out around the table and Rico chuckled.

"Well, now you know the Board members of The Farmington Corporation. You are the only one who has ever seen us all in one place, outside the staff of Farmington. As for Benjamin, they don't know about us, but we know all about him."

Rico's tone turned serious. "You aren't the only one taking a trust risk here. The men around this table are the seeds planted by The Farm to come here and do today what those men did for us. Your betrayal could bring our operation down and sever our connections with The Commune."

Turning to Jason he said, "We're taking a risk too. If our connection with The Commune is severed, we don't have many options for providing medicine and treatments to those who can't afford them."

"I'm betting on the man I knew a long time ago, that he still has the same integrity and instincts that I trusted my life with."

Turning to The Board, he said, "Let's give him the deep dive into our operations. Antonio and Derrell, let him see the files on Benjamin, he may need that information for leverage if things go off the rails. Ross, show him the tunnels first. Jason, I'll see you back here in two hours."

"This Board Meeting is adjourned."

The men around the table dispersed.

Nicholas didn't believe it could be this easy. Sitting in the green space of his quarters he savored the sunshine and the scheme he and Benjamin had created. *What was the name?* he thought. *Oh yes, Operation External Affairs.* He took a sip of the mint nectar tea and closed his eyes. There it was again, that little thought that something was wrong.He shrugged it off. Jason was taking to the idea of being involved in the activities of Outside with little prompting from him. Nicholas could feign innocence to Althea. "I didn't know what he and Benjamin were doing," he practiced.

There it was again, that feeling. He thought of Althea and the sick feeling came back. *This would break her,* he thought. While he didn't agree with her decision to awaken the relative, she was his mother. Nicholas had not thought ahead about how his betrayal would affect Althea. Rather than retire to the Community of Elders and Children, she would be forced into the Community of Transition. How would she fare, not having the responsibility for leading their family? The reality of his plans coming to fruition had a surprising effect on Nicholas – he wanted the comfort and advice of his mother.

althea

Althea took the long way around to the Commune of Elders and Children where she sat on a nearby bench. She knew the schedule, and this was science time. The children were outside on a "discovery mission." The point of the mission was to see what things in nature piqued the young learners' interests. Althea held back a chuckle as she saw one adventurer discover a fat grasshopper and share it with his teacher. The woman coughed to hide her startled reaction and then encouraged the boy to let the grasshopper go about its mission. That instructor must have been substituting for the regular science instructor.

She didn't do it often, but Althea occasionally visited to just sit in this Commune. The Commune of Elders and Children felt different than any place in the entire Commune of African Descendants. There was freedom for the children to be joyful and inquisitive; to experience both the thrill of adventure and the security of home and relationships. Those who taught the children were all over 50 years of age, so learners got the benefits of both knowledge and wisdom.

While the children looked forward to time in The Commune, it was the Instructors who believed they were the greatest beneficiaries. After devoting their lives in service to work, research or Family Leadership, they were honored with the responsibility of sharing all they knew with future generations.

Most curriculum used within The Commune of Elders and Children was based on the experience and insights of the teachers. The learning center had a peer review system that insured instructors were placed with students and in disciplines where their skill and passions aligned. Learning pods consisted of no more than eight children assigned to one instructor for a period of time. Younger children were in pods three months at a time, while older children spent longer time in their learning pods. Younger children were assigned to pods based on temperament and intellectual interests. Older children's pods included learning designed to meet the projected needs of the larger Commune.

Althea's thoughts went to her family. She would not be able to join this Commune if her family was in disarray. Though she had seen signs of a warming between Nicholas and Jason, her instincts told her something was off. Nicholas' desire to keep The Commune financially safe from the influences of Outside was admirable, but Althea believed his approach left no time for family business. How could he effectively serve as Family Elder if business was more important than family? And if Nicholas did not become Family Elder, who would take on that role? Jason didn't know enough about their lives here, and other members of the family would not support an elder from Before.

Althea looked to the far end of The Commune of Elders and Children where one of the older children's learning pods had gathered for an intellectual discussion.

Civil debate was encouraged in learning, but the children might be uncomfortable debating in front of one not part of their learning environment.

She rose to her feet, taking a breath filled with regret. Althea turned and walked slowly back towards her obligations and family's dwelling, realizing that her dream of transitioning to the Commune of Elders and Children was getting further away.

nicholas

Nicholas watched as his mother walked to their family's quarters. He could tell that she was coming from the Commune of Elders and Children by the slow, tearful steps she took. Althea tried to hide her sadness, but he knew her.

When did their relationship get so stormy? He remembered the songs she sang when he had nightmares after his father died. He realized now that as he drifted off to sleep as a child, Althea had also cried during the lullabies. His mother had been his whole world until he was 17. That is when the assumption of his training for Family Elder was to start. There were other families who also trained their eldest children in preparation to assume the role of Family Elder, but none of them had Althea's influence and respect.

When Benjamin started to take an interest in his growth, Nicholas was flattered.Initially, Althea also consented to Nicholas learning from Benjamin. Something changed, though, when Althea rejected Benjamin as a suitor.

Benjamin pursued a relationship with Nicholas even more, while Althea became guarded in her support of Benjamin's relationship with her son. She gently encouraged Nicholas to pursue the mathematics and engineering leadership tract because he was able to identify the components necessary to build. This, Althea told him often, would be useful to the Commune's expansion in the future. The more she talked with him, the more Nicholas insisted on being mentored by Benjamin. In their last argument about Benjamin, Althea confessed that she didn't trust Benjamin's motives or dealings in business.

And then Althea never spoke to Nicholas about Benjamin again.

Althea had been right. Nicholas had seen and learned things about Benjamin's business dealings outside that he knew were outside Commune standards. Benjamin said to Nicholas and his sons often, "Our work outside is insurance for the future survival of the Commune. If the powers that be ever come to take us over, we are building other options." On the surface it sounded good, but one of the Commune of African Descendant's principles was: We are led and function by the Ruach, not situational ethics.

Nicholas sensed the Wind now as he thought of his mother's sacrifices for their Commune. He closed his eyes and pictured the young widow, and the older woman who only wanted to teach future generations. In his determination to prove himself ready to be the Family Elder, Nicholas had done just the opposite – he had behaved like a petulant child.

Nicholas realized he wanted Althea to have the peace and joy she deserved in the Commune of Elders and Children, more than he even wanted to be Family Elder. It was time to talk with his mother about his involvement with Benjamin's outside work.

chapter 54: connections

Hester waited for Jason to arrive at their meeting spot. He was late, and that was unusual. As she considered whether to go home, she saw him hurrying through the pathway. Hester smiled. That rush thing he did always struck her as funny. The culture here was one of relaxed efficiency. If one was late, there must be a good reason, so why try to make up for time that was already gone? For an individual to be late as a matter of character was unheard of.

Jason arrived at the park, still breathing heavily.

"I'm so sorry," he started.

"Please stop talking and breathe," Hester said laughing, "I have time for you."

She sat down.

Sitting beside her, Jason took a few deep breaths and felt himself calm. He liked the peaceful state he had come to associate with Hester.

He looked at her, "How was your day?"

Smiling, Hester told him about a theory she was exploring about a new natural fertilizer. Then she abruptly changed subjects, telling Jason that her father had asked what he was learning.

"That is a great segue for talking about my day. I got to speak with my friend Rico and meet his team. There is so much I have to tell you."

Hester leaned forward, "Tell me everything," she said.

Jason did just that.

farmington corporation

Derrell, Antonio, and Jim Bob came into Rico's office.

"Well, we have some information you need to know. This might give you the leverage you need with Benjamin, but tipping our hands could be dangerous."

Rico nodded. "What do you have?," he asked.

Derrell started. "I'll get to the puzzle first. Benjamin's citizenship documents for The Commune are forged. He seems to have been somehow inserted into one of the leading families by FFI."

Derrell held up his hand. "Before you ask, it gets better. Benjamin is not from now, he's from Before, like us."

Rico leaned forward. "You're not finished explaining, right?

Jim Bob continued, "You know how files that don't match up to regular data get flagged? Well, Benjamin has lots of them. He shows up in our files as belonging to Farmington, but there's a three-way lock on the information. Here's the deep part: the first part of the lock is from the original Farm organization.The second part of the lock is from FFI, and the final part came from within our own organization. Someone inside the beginning of Farmington Corporation created a failsafe file on Benjamin, that if accessed will shut down our entire network."

Rico exploded, "And we're just finding this out? This man has been supplying us with resources from inside The Commune, and he's, one, not legitimately a family member there, two, from Before, and three, somehow tied to the beginnings of our organization?"

Rico's voice changed from explosive to quiet and menacing. "Do you gentlemen know what this means? It means Benjamin knows a lot more about us than we do about him. It means we find out who he is, why those old men decided he was worth keeping a secret, and why FFI planted him in The Commune? I never trusted that guy. We have a man on the inside now. Get with Isaiah and let's set up a way to get to Jason inside the Commune."

chapter 55: the farm

The leaders of each farm sat with Ben Goodwin. He shared his report on the financial health of each of the Farm properties. At the rate they were going, The Farm would be able to purchase additional land in the Western US to create five additional Farms. They discussed the future, creating communities for women and investing in industries other than farming. It had taken The Farm Network ten years to go from nothing to having eight farms and changing the lives of countless Black men. A couple of the old ones that started with them had passed on, but they had been succeeded by men who were just as committed.

Ben Goodwin believed his work with The Farm was important and it had changed his life. For the first time he was a part of something positive. As he drove home after the meeting, he noticed the police lights on an unmarked car behind him. The driver of the car pulled alongside him and gestured for him to pull over. Ben was surprised. He hadn't been involved in any illegal activities in years. The work he did with The Farm was secret, but not illegal. He pulled over and waited nervously.

A masked and uniformed officer got out of the car and gestured for him to get out. After patting him down, the officer led Ben to the back of the unmarked car and said firmly, "Get in." Ben didn't see much choice. These types of officers made regular people disappear. To his surprise, in the backseat of the car were two of the congressmen from his state.

"We want to talk with you about The Farm," one of them said.

Driving back home, Ben was conflicted. Had he really sold out The Farm Network, or was the government already aware of them, and coming to shut them down? He remembered being frightened because of what they knew about him and could do with that knowledge. Yes, he gave them the locations of each Farm, but he didn't tell them how many men were there, or how much money the network had. They seemed to know a lot already and only needed him to confirm.

He knew they were sending men to shut down The Farm Network. The politicians said the Farm Network was a threat to current plans and the societal balance needed to keep things moving. Ben knew bull when he heard it, but he had a family to consider. He had a new life away from the one he had before. He wasn't willing to risk his life or his family for anyone.

On the day it happened, The Farm implemented its failsafe: each Farm's "Seed" was driven to FFI with papers identifying them as the son of an FFI Investor. The seeds would be sent to the future to continue the mission of The Farm. Ben had been planted as a shadow board member of FFI; one who would never attend a meeting, but whose seat had been purchased by The Farm. Ben's responsibility as a shadow board member of FFI was to insure all The Farm's seeds had paperwork that would qualify them for the program. Whether through influence or bribery, each seed had to make it into the program, and ultimately to the future.

On the day the government invaded the Farm Network, Ben heard shots, then silence over the communication devices as one farm after another fell to "authorized representatives." These representatives were apparently authorized to confiscate the land, steal the equipment and murder those still present.

It started with a single match at the North Carolina farm. Most of the men were asleep, except for those who were on watch. Winston heard a loud pop and the sound of a truck pulling away real fast. He knew that wasn't good. Running to the end of the men's dormitory, he looked out and saw a bright blaze burning. Harvey and a couple of the men from inside the house had also heard the pop and came outside to the burning flames. *What if this was random?,* they wondered. *What if they didn't mean to take the Farm Network down?*

As the men speculated about the source of the attack, they heard gunshots and the violent maniacal laughter of men invading the property. Do they fight or assume the worst? Harvey was responsible for communications at the North Carolina Farm. He placed one cryptic message to the Farm's mobile network: "Alert: Invaders. Hoods. NC Black."

Winston woke the men in the barracks, telling them what happened. He said quickly here's your choice: stay and fight or take your chances and run. Most of the men ran. However, five men, reputed killers from the streets of Chicago, who had been given a new chance at life, fought to the death alongside the four old men attempting to protect the North Carolina Farm.

George was the first to get taken down by an invaders bullet. He was young, 17. The Old Ones had spotted his false courage when he first arrived. Winston stopped for a second to remember the day the man's façade dropped. The day he stopped pretending was the day he became a man. What George lacked in smarts, he made up in unabashed enthusiasm. *Damn,* he thought, *George would have been one of their proudest accomplishments.*

Instantly Winston was back in the present. "Spread out! We're in their range," he yelled to the others.

Winston remembered his father telling them about the night riders and how they ran through and burned farms, laughing and shooting and drinking. As a little boy hearing this, Winston was frightened. But now he was just angry –– angrier than he thought he could ever be. It wasn't enough to exclude our people, our kids, from the opportunities to make money. But when someone found a way to turn their lives around, just like in Tulsa or Rosewood or other towns, these hate-fueled savages found a way to kill it. Winston loaded the rifle again, pointed in the direction where one of the invaders was running and squeezed. The invader fell. Winston took out two more before he felt the hammer hit the back of his head. His last thought as a human being, *I'm going to have these tears now.*

One by one, Ben heard variations of the same message come across the Farm's mobile network:

"Alert: Invaders. Hoods. Mississippi black."

"Alert: We got a few groups of Invaders here. Y'all must have pissed 'em off Mississippi. Georgia going black."

"Alert: I think they got some more joiners here too. Don't think we can hold 'em. Tennessee black."

"Alert: They're here too. This was a coordinated attack. Been my honor brothers. Alabama black."

"This Louisiana's alert. They're here too. OK, you look out now. You're the last man standing. Bye y'all. Louisiana black."

"Alert: Hey Brothers. We did good work. I'm gonna lay down knowing we did our part.Oklahoma black. God help this country."

Ben heard every announcement. He heard the gunshots in the background and the cries of men who had only tried to do good.The static between the alerts had been comforting. As long as there was static, someone was still on the line. After the Oklahoma alert, the silence of the Farm Network made Ben cry aloud in anguish. It was over.

As The Farm's accountant, Ben wasn't assigned to any one farm, but he was responsible to them all. At his home in Detroit, Ben felt sick with grief for the loss of The Farm Network, and the role he had played in its demise. He took a drink and waited for the calls.

Three hours later, Ben had started to wonder if the plan had failed, when the phone started ringing. The calls came every 20 minutes and as he met each Farm Lead, the phone rang signaling the next meeting. There was a longer interval as Ben waited for the last call.

"Hello," he said. The voice on the other end said, "Meet me at the designated spot in one hour. Bring the documents."

Ben received seven calls that night and met each Farm leader at a predetermined location in Detroit. One by one, Ben provided the qualifying paperwork for each Seed's participation in the cryotechnology program of FFI. Each meeting was painful for him, but this last meeting was the most convicting.

Ben got in the car with Henry. Henry was disappointed, hurt and something else.The man's piercing glance told Ben that Henry suspected his involvement.

"This attack was precise and coordinated; someone inside must have betrayed The Network," Henry said.

Each Farm had planned for the day this could happen and had done the advance work to prepare for it, but it still hurt. The elders who had given land, identified and snatched their own off the streets, and worked The Farm network, had done their best. Now they, like everyone else, placed their hope in the future. Henry had confided to the other leaders that he didn't trust the accountant. The man could never look him in the eyes. His father always told him that a man who can't look another man in the eyes is hiding something. It was a bitter irony that Henry was right. He stared at Ben for what seemed like hours, until the man in the backseat, the Seed Henry was responsible for, cleared his throat. This meeting was the final step in dissolving The Farm today and preparing for tomorrow.

Inside the folder were the signed forms transferring all the finances of The Farm Network to Ben, who would set up the future Farmington Corporation.

In addition, there was also an identity that would take Ben into the future to wake up the seeds at the right time. After waking the seeds, Ben's work would be done, and he had agreed to disappear for an independent life in the future.

Henry didn't say goodbye but stared at the man a while longer. This was all personal to him. He hoped they had put their trust in the right man. If not, none of what they tried to do would matter. "You can get out now," Henry said unceremoniously.

Ben blinked and realized the man was serious. He felt like there should have been some final words between them, but Henry was done talking. Tears welled up in Ben's eyes as the old man reached over and opened the door, "Leave," he said.

Ben stood in the parking lot, holding the folder with all the documents that would ensure The Farm lived on, and that he would too.

the future
chapter 56: jason

After his talk with Hester, Jason was somewhat calmer. His thoughts were still racing. Understanding what Benjamin had done to his own brother, and now learning of the activities outside the Commune he was involved in validated the alarm bells the man set off in him. Jason wondered though, was Nicholas a willing participant or an expendable accomplice? If Nicholas was involved, knowing how Benjamin's plans would affect his own mother, the man was even worse than Benjamin. He wasn't sure what to do next, or how to move forward. He wondered if he should talk with Althea or Laura. Jason was conflicted; he wanted to warn Althea about what Benjamin and Nicholas were doing, but he knew it would break her heart. Just as he decided which woman he would speak with, he heard a bird whistling outside his window.

Jason walked over to the window curiously and saw a bird perched on the arm of the chair. Friendly birds weren't anything new here, but this bird didn't move as Jason eyed it. The bird suddenly flew into Jason's quarters and perched upon his desk. Then he heard Rico's voice:

"Don't be scared, J. It's me. We call this comms invention The Little Birdie. Cute huh?" Rico continued. "We use it for intelligence in places we can't just walk into. I'm looking at you and I know it feels weird, but I could only speak if we knew you were alone." Rico went on, "I'm here with two of the board members you met earlier today.

They have some information about your guy Benjamin that could explain both of our bad feelings about him. Can you talk now? Oh, you don't have to sit with that dumbfounded look on your face; go on, speak to the little birdie, Jason.It won't bite."

Jason heard the other men laughing softly in the background.

"Every time I think I'm getting my bearings here, some other strange thing happens," Jason started.

Despite the distance and time, he knew that Rico was still the man he could trust more than anyone else in this time. "Tell me what you know."

"Where should I start?", Rico asked. "Here or 240 years ago? For this conversation, you're going to need a discreet trip here. Do you think you can get away without Benjamin knowing?"

Jason hesitated. "If this conversation is as important as you say it is, I might need to bring someone with me."

laura

"Auntie," Jason started. "I have been observing the traditions and understand your position as a member of the Justice Circle. I would like to make an appeal to go outside The Commune. I believe I have information that would greatly impact the safety of The Commune but understand that as a new son I am forbidden to leave without permission."

"What do you propose, my son?" Jason realized that Laura had reverted to the formal language and followed her lead.

"I ask that you, as a member of the Justice Circle, or whomever you designate, accompany me to a meeting with The Farmington Corporation to hear information they have on an influential member of The Commune of African Descendants."

"Does the information you allude to directly impact me or my family?", Laura asked.

"Yes, Auntie, the information directly impacts you and your family."Then I am forbidden to go. I will assign one on the council known as The Protector to go with you. He will hear and discern clearly and see to it that you are protected from punishment.When would you like to leave?"

"Auntie, I would like to leave now."

collision

Jason sat unhooded as he drove to Farmington Corporation for the first time. He was surprised how familiar these futuristic streets looked to the ones he remembered from Before. There was the same despair he remembered from the streets. He sensed the walls around certain areas indicated the prosperous areas. He shook his head, and a sad chuckle escaped his mouth.

"The Protector" looked at him. "Is something wrong, my son?"

Jason looked at the man. He looked like he was fierce enough to protect some stuff. But there was also a quiet dignity about the man that invited Jason to share his thoughts.

"I was looking at the streets here and remembering the ones from my time. Things out here don't seem to have changed much."

The Protector studied him for a minute. "Change can only happen when societies are willing to embrace it. If the work of becoming mentally, financially and spiritually whole is done, change is the likely outcome. The streets look the same because the mind of a people must change before their streets do." The Protector continued, "And to be clear, This is your time. You came from another, but here is where you are. Are you able to embrace the change required to live in this here and now?"

Jason looked at The Protector and replied, "I don't know."

"Then you must honestly evaluate your ability to embrace change, or return to what is familiar," The Protector responded, ending the conversation.

The transporter vehicle stopped in front of The Farmington Corporation, and The Protector exited the vehicle first, walking through the doors like he owned the place. Jason fell in step behind. When they arrived at the reception desk, the woman said, "They're already in the board room."

Rico stood at the head of the table and gestured for the two men to have seats on his left hand. After introductions were made, Rico asked Antonio, head of security to begin the presentation. The presentation introduced all in the room to Benjamin, AKA Ben, shadow member of the Board of FFI, and accountant to the former Farm Network.

The presentation included details of all financial dealings with The Farmington Corporation and shadow pharmacies and doctors. The final nails in the coffin included his taking the place of a legitimate Commune Elder and then bribing a doctor to create a fake medical report for Raphael, the legitimate Elder for their clan. The information collected and presented would rival any CIA intelligence file.

After the presentation, Rico stated, "Gentlemen what you do with this information is up to you. For the sake of an old brotherhood," he nodded to Jason, "I thought it would be good to have this information."

The Protector rose, his face unreadable."Thank you for your concern for The Commune of African Descendants. Would some members of your team be willing to accompany us back and sit before the Circle of Justice with this information?"

Rico smiled as Derrell and Antonio rose to join him."Your car or mine?"

not your ordinary courthouse

Jason realized that he was being given the privilege to see something few in the Commune of African descendants had seen.Not only was he here, but his friend Rico was here. He saw Hester and moved to take a seat in the back with her. He introduced Hester to Rico, Antonio and Derrell. For the first time since waking up in this time, things felt right. He was literally introducing his hoped-for future to his past. He considered The Protector's words about doing the work of becoming whole enough to live in *this time.*

He decided, looking at his best friend and Hester, that this time is *his time*.

The members of the Circle of Justice entered the room and took their assigned places in the semi-circle at the front of the room. There was a regalness about them; each seemed to bring a spirit into the room that was calming, fair and right. They had heard the evidence presented by the Farmington Corporation and had their discussion behind closed doors. Whether they argued or fought, no one would ever know. When the Circle of Justice entered the Justice Hall, they were united in their decision.

"Please summon Elder Benjamin," The Protector said in a deep, soft voice.

reunion

Laura sat across from Jason later that afternoon and noticed a tear streaming down her face."It was over," she thought to herself. The information Farmington Corporation provided about Benjamin's involvement in the outside underworld was one thing. The proof of Benjamin's papers being fabricated sealed everything.Raphael, her love who had been falsely assigned to life as a transitioning, mentally deficient senior, was the rightful Elder to their clan. Jason's contacts from the Farmington Corporation had provided proof of every malfeasance. Raphael was coming home. The Commune of African Descendants owed a great debt to The Farmington Corporation.

The evidence compiled against Benjamin over the years by The Farmington Corporation was enough to exile him from The Commune of African Descendants. Not only would Benjamin be exiled, but so would his family. If Benjamin's documents had been fabricated, all those attached to him were also questionable. There would be a ceremony of mourning for the identity of the relative Benjamin had taken. The circle of past to future must be closed.

chapter 57: justice delayed

The members of the Justice Forward Circle and the Council of Families accompanied Benjamin and his family to the edge of The Commune of African Descendants. His work on the outside had flagrantly violated the Commune's principles. In addition, the ethical breaches he used to undermine Raphael's leadership as Chief Elder of the Commune sealed his fate, and those of his family. The information provided by Rico and the Farmington Corporation showed that Benjamin, or Ben Morris from Before, had colluded with FFI to assume the identity of a never-wakened relative of Raphael. He was never a member of the Commune.

Benjamin's crimes would never have been discovered if not for something none of them could have anticipated: the newly awakened Jason and Richard, formerly known as Rico, having a bond that stretched across time. The information provided by Rico to Jason and The Commune identified Benjamin as the accountant for the Farm who was supposed to wake the Seeds and disappear into obscurity.Instead, the former accountant had attempted to take over The Commune of African Descendants while establishing a criminal enterprise Outside.

Nicholas was able to corroborate the information provided by Rico because of his close work with Benjamin. Nicholas had also knowingly violated Commune Principles in the work he did with Benjamin.

Because he provided information to help convict Benjamin and vindicate Raphael, Nicholas was given leniency by the Justice Forward Circle. However, because of his involvement the Council of Families concluded that Nicholas could never be named Family Elder.

Althea watched the sun rise with a bittersweet heart.She had her son back. When he came to her to confess all that Benjamin was doing and his involvement, she knew that he would never be Family Elder.That was ok. Nicholas apologized and realized what had motivated his behavior: a striving to get ahead that ignored the wisdom necessary to lead. They had talked long into the night, and Althea helped him understand the consequences of his actions. Nicholas' heart had changed, and he said he was ready to be the person the Commune needed, even if that wasn't Family Elder. That was the bitter part.

The sweet part was that today was her last day as Family Elder in the Council of Families. Althea was finally going to the Commune of Elders and Children. Her heart felt like it was bursting with joy. The Family Elder of the Chibuzo clan had been named their Family Elder to the Council. Nicholas was gracious as he stood with Althea to affirm their family's support of the new Elder.

one year later
conclusion: accepted and beloved

The energy in the Commune of African Descendants was electric with excitement. Jason, the new son, was being welcomed into their community as one of their own.Jason knelt in front of Raphael, Chief Elder of The Families. As he looked up into the older man's face, he noticed the man's eyes were smiling through tears. The man expressed his gratitude to Kamva for restoring not only his position, but his family. Jason's new name in the Commune of African Descendants was Kamva, meaning, "the future." Kamva lowered his head to receive the blessing of not just an elder, but a father.

Kamva was also being wed to Hester today. As their nuptials ended, The Elders from each family in the Commune surrounded the couple to bless their union and children. It felt magical and beautiful, and the Ruach Wind blew over the couple and all who were gathered in the Council of African Descendants. In a break from every tradition, Rico was allowed inside The Commune to witness the adoption of Kamva into the Commune of African Descendants, and to stand with the new groom as he wed Hester.

jason

Letter to the past...

I have lived in the time called Before, and in this present time which back then would be the Future. As I sit in my quarters, pondering the difference between then and now, I remember Grandma Ruby and her desire to shield me from the harshness of that world. Your time is hard. Those old men knew it and did what they could to prepare us. The idea that the elders would surrender their land to be used as training for the future is still brilliant, even by the standards in 2201. What kind of "old woman" would bet everything she had on the future? I realize Grandma Ruby and the elders of Before had sight beyond what many in that time gave them credit for. How might my life be different if I had sat with her and learned rather than simply making money to pay for her life? The mindset to get money was so strong back then that we surrendered other things in our pursuit of it. I wish I had spent more time with her.

When Grandma Ruby found out I was in the childcare system because I didn't have parents – no, that wasn't right. I was there because my parents either couldn't or wouldn't care for me.

Jason stopped writing, closed his eyes, and looked further back in time. His imagination seemed to be set ablaze by the Ruach. He felt the evil hopelessness of the slave ships, the terror of families whose fathers had been lynched, and the rushed journeys of flight to the north where a different kind of oppression waited.

He began to write again.

The spirit that provoked these events was pure, ancient evil; thinly veiled worship of Mammon. Of course, Mammon had accomplices. Racism was the leading principality that served Mammon in the U.S. While not as strong because of the work in the Commune of African Descendants, racism still seeks to influence how humans interact with each other now in 2201. What started as the capture and import of human labor created a system where some gave themselves the right to take and own others based on man-made constructs like race. What is the solution for those whose brilliance has changed the world?

Community. A place where each gift and spark of brilliance can be nurtured until it grows into innovation that sustains that same community. A place where safety isn't accomplished by moving away, but by moving towards each other. Respect. Before the elders were shunned aside. Here, they provide a safe place to learn and to be. Children deserve the chance to be children, to ask questions, and to be taught in a loving, safe environment.   Look to the elders. Take care of the children. Create the Community that eliminates fear. You have to. For the future.

Jason closed his eyes and remembered the laughter that came from the learning pods in the Community of Elders and Children. He saw the faces of Grandma Ruby and Althea. He remembered the lessons from old men from The Farm. Those old men still existed not just in Farmington Corporation, but in Jason. They had shown him how to change in the past, and now they were with him here in the future.

What gives a story power? If you are a reader there are some stories you've read that have changed your perspective on life. Perhaps it was the hero's journey through circumstances that challenged his or her inward purpose and gave you courage to try yourself. Maybe it was reading about the childhood trauma of a well-known person that gave you the strength to fight for your own peace.

The fight in a story unveils the strength of the leading character. What fight are you currently experiencing? Where in your mind, body or spirit do you feel the effects of that fight? Shift your eyes for a moment. What is in you that will win the fight? Here's where you have to break from the norms of your existence: don't look at what others have done in similar circumstances. Quiet your thoughts and see the story from the perspective of its Author. What might the Author be attempting to accomplish through your story?

For far too long our stories have been used as sources of shame, entertainment, or fuel for anger and its byproducts (mistaken identity, mayhem and murder). Stop for a minute and consider your own story. Here's another question to consider: what has shifted in your story? What event, person or set of circumstances are you experiencing that can change where your story is going?

Jason's story changed. He went from a societally prepared script for how his life would go, to a series of events that disrupted life as he knew it. Some of those factors included systemic racism, a lack of generational preparedness, and few options from his perspective. Vision disrupted Jason's story: his grandmother's vision of what could become of him if he stayed on the same path. Vision was also present in the old men of The Farm.

The collision of the factors above, along with changing societal standards, profit-above-people thinking and innovation created the pathway to something completely different. All of the factors in these life collisions aren't bad. Ruby had to make a courageous choice that cost her everything. The vision from the old men included mentorship. FFI, even with its methods, added innovation. Every character's choices led to Jason's new story. The story didn't have to have a happy ending; Jason also had to choose which direction his story would take.

How might your story shape the future? What elements in your story point to the solutions you have been uniquely crafted to bring to the world? What problem have you successfully solved? What is the problem your heart longs to solve? Quiet the noise around you until you can hear the Author's heart beating the solution of the problem you have been created to solve.

Althea, with all of her influence and positioning, had a deep desire to nurture the next generation of leaders.

In the writing of 2200, I envisioned a community where everyone's gifts were used to benefit the entire community. Age was not a barrier to effective contribution. Business acumen was not just used to make oneself profitable, but to identify solutions that build community. Don't misunderstand, we should profit from the work of our hands, but profit is not the end result of your hands' work; change is.

Whose story have you written off because they are too old? In The Commune of African Descendants age was a cause for celebration and contribution, not a reason to minimize. There is still vision in your mother, your father, your grandparents and aunties.

Whose story have you minimized because they are too young? The times we live in are causing children to grow up fast and often broken. The 'adultification' of Black children is well documented, causing them to be treated as adults and given harsher treatments at a younger age. In *2200*, children are allowed to play, be curious, and safely explore intellectual differences according to their individual and collective makeup. They are guarded by the oldest in the Commune because they are the most precious cargo in our communities.

I may not be quite ready for the Commune of Elders and Children. But while I wait, I pray I can tell stories that point to a world that is safe for us all.

You are loved,

Michele

about the author

Michele Aikens is an author, coach, and compassionate voice to leaders navigating crisis, burnout or transition. Known for her spiritual discernment and deeply encouraging presence, she helps leaders realign with purpose and lead from a place of wholeness.

Aikens is a certified and credentialed coach through the International Coaching Federation (ICF) and holds a master's degree in organizational leadership. As CEO of Clear Sight Coaching & Consulting, Inc., she guides individuals and teams with wisdom, grace, and prophetic clarity.

Connect with her at **www.itspossible.today** or **www.clearsight-coach.com**.

other books by the author

Not Just Any Kind of Woman

Not Just Any Kind of Woman: The Middle Years

The Homecoming:
A Story for Anyone Who Has Ever Lost His Way

Last Night I Dreamed My Purpose (Children's Book)

Consider the Possibilities: Pursuing What Matters Most

www.ingramcontent.com/pod-product-compliance
Lightning Source LLC
Chambersburg PA
CBHW040530170726
48295CB00012B/409